G.F Browne

The Christian Church in these Islands before the coming of Augustine

G.F Browne

The Christian Church in these Islands before the coming of Augustine

1st Edition | ISBN: 978-3-75237-790-3

Place of Publication: Frankfurt am Main, Germany

Year of Publication: 2020

Outlook Verlag GmbH, Germany.

Reproduction of the original.

THE CHRISTIAN CHURCH IN THESE ISLANDS BEFORE THE COMING OF AUGUSTINE.

BY THE

REV. G. F. BROWNE

LECTURE I.

Importance of the anniversaries connected with the years 1894-1897.—Christianity in Kent immediately before Augustine.—Dates of Bishop Luidhard and Queen Bertha.—Romano-British Churches in Canterbury.—Who were the Britons.—Traditional origin of British Christianity.—St. Paul.—Joseph of Arimathea.—Glastonbury.—Roman references to Britain.

We are approaching an anniversary of the highest interest to all English people: to English Churchmen first, for it is the thirteen-hundredth anniversary of the planting of the Church of England; but also to all who are proud of English civilisation, for the planting of a Christian Church is the surest means of civilisation, and English civilisation owes everything to the English Church. In 1897 those who are still here will celebrate the thirteen-hundredth anniversary of the conversion of Ethelbert, king of the Kentish people, by Augustine and the band of missionaries sent by our great benefactor Gregory, the sixty-fourth bishop of Rome. I am sorry that the limitation of my present subject prevents me from enlarging upon the merits of that great man, and upon our debt to him. Englishmen must always remember that it was Gregory who gave to the Italian Mission whatever force it had; it was Gregory who gave it courage, when the dangers of a journey through France were sufficient to keep it for months shivering with fear under the shadow of the Alps; it was Gregory who gave it such measure of wisdom and common sense as it had, qualities which its leader sadly lacked. Coming nearer to the present year, there will be in 1896 the final departure of Augustine from Rome to commemorate, on July 23, and his arrival here in the late autumn. In 1895 there will be to commemorate the first departure from Rome of Augustine and his Mission, by way of Lérins and Marseilles to Aix, and the return of Augustine to Rome, when his companions, in fear of the dangers of the way, refused to go further. An ill-omened beginning, prophetic and prolific of like results. The history of the Italian Mission is a history of failure to face danger. Mellitus fled from London, and got himself safe to Gaul; Justus fled from Rochester, and got himself safe to Gaul; Laurentius was packed up to fly from Canterbury and follow them[1]; Paulinus fled from York. In 1894 we have, as I believe, to commemorate the final abandonment of earlier and independent plans for the conversion of the English in Kent, from which abandonment the Mission of Augustine came to be.

It is a very interesting fact that just when we are preparing to commemorate the thirteen-hundredth anniversary of the introduction of Christianity into England, and are drawing special attention to the fact that Christianity had existed in this island, among the Britons, for at least four hundred years before its introduction to the English, our neighbours in France are similarly engaged. They are preparing to celebrate in 1896 the fourteen-hundredth anniversary of "the introduction of Christianity into France," as the newspapers put it. This means that in 496, Clovis, king of the Franks, became a Christian; as, in 597, Ethelbert, king of the Kentish-men, became a Christian[2]. As we have to keep very clear in our minds the distinction between the introduction of Christianity among the English, from whom the country is called England, and its introduction long before into Britain; so our continental neighbours have to keep very clear the difference between the introduction of Christianity among the Franks, from whom the country is called France, and its introduction long before into Gaul. The Archbishop of Rheims, whose predecessor Remigius baptized Clovis in 496, is arranging a solemn celebration of their great anniversary; and the Pope has accorded a six months' jubilee in honour of the occasion. No doubt the Archbishop of Canterbury, whose predecessor Augustine baptized Ethelbert, will in like manner make arrangements for a solemn celebration of our great anniversary. It would be an interesting and fitting thing, to hold a thanksgiving service within the walls of Richborough, which is generally accepted as the scene of Augustine's first interview with King Ethelbert, and has now been secured and put into the hands of trustees[3]. The two commemorations, at Rheims and at Canterbury, are linked together in a special way by the fact that Clotilde, the Christian wife of Clovis, was the great-grandmother of Bertha, the Christian wife of Ethelbert.

In the year 594, two years before the arrival of Augustine, there was, and I believe had long been, a Christian queen in pagan Kent; there was, and I believe had long been, a Christian bishop in pagan Canterbury, sent there to minister to the Christian queen. An excellent opening this for the conversion of the king and people, an opening intentionally created by those who made the marriage on the queen's side. But, however hopeful the opening, the immediate result was disappointing. If more of missionary help had been sent from Gaul, from whence this bishop came, the conversion of the king and people might have come in the natural way, by an inflow of Christianity from the neighbouring country. But such help, though pressingly asked for, was not given; and as I read such signs as there are, this year 594, of which we now inaugurate the thirteen-hundredth anniversary, was the year in which it came home to those chiefly concerned that the conversion was not to be effected by the means adopted. Beyond some very limited area of Christianity, only the queen and some few of her people, and the religious services maintained for them, the bishop's work was to be barren. The limited work which he did was that for which ostensibly he had come; but I think we are meant to understand that his Christian ambition was larger than this, his Christian hope higher. I shall make no apology for dwelling a little upon the circumstances of this Christian work, immediately before the coming of Augustine. It may seem a little discursive; but it forms, I think, a convenient introduction to our general subject.

Who Bishop Luidhard was, is a difficult question. That he came from Gaul is certain, but his name is clearly Teutonic; whence, perhaps, his acceptability as a visitor to the English. He has been described as Bishop of Soissons; but the lists of bishops there make no mention of him, nor do the learned authors and compilers of *Gallia Christiana*. This assignment of Luidhard to the bishopric of Soissons may perhaps be explained by an interesting story.

The Bishop of Soissons, a full generation earlier than the time of which we are speaking, was Bandaridus. He was charged before King Clotaire, that one of the four sons of the first Clovis who succeeded to the kingdom called "of Soissons," with many offences of many kinds; and he was banished. He crossed over to England—for so Britain is described in the old account—and there lived in a monastery for seven years, performing the humble functions of a kitchen-gardener. Whether the story is sufficiently historical to enable us to claim the continuance of Christian monasteries of the British among the barbarian Saxons so late as 540, I am not clear. There was a little Irish monastery at Bosham, among the pagan South-Saxons, a hundred and forty years later. It is easy, I think, to overrate the hostility of the early English to Christianity. Penda of Mercia has the character of being murderously hostile; but it was land, not creed, that he cared for. He was quite broad and undenominational in his slaughters.

About A. D. 545, a great plague raged at Soissons, and the people begged for the return of their bishop. He went back to his old charge, and there is no suggestion that he ever left it again. This legend of a Bishop of Soissons coming to our island, may well have given rise to the tradition that Bishop Luidhard, who certainly was living in the time of Bandaridus, had been Bishop of Soissons. In any case, the incidental hint the story gives us of the skill of our neighbours on the continent in the cultivation of vegetables, even at that early time, makes the story worth reproduction. The Bishop of Soissons, at the time of which we are speaking, was Droctigisilus (variously spelled, as might perhaps be expected). Of him Gregory of Tours tells that he lost his senses through over-drinking. Gregory adds a moral reflection—if we can so describe it—which does not give us a very high idea of the practical

Christianity of the times. It is this:—"Though he was a voracious eater, and drank immoderately, exceeding the bounds which priestly caution should impose, no one ever accused him of adultery[4]." If we must choose a bishop of Soissons to be represented by Luidhard, we may fairly prefer the vegetable-gardener to the immoderate drinker.

We read, again, in fairly early times, that our first Christian bishop in England had been bishop of Senlis. The authors and compilers of *Gallia Christiana* insert the name of Lethardus, or Letaldus, among the bishops of Senlis, quoting Sprot and Thorn. He was said to have come over with Bertha as early as 566, and they insert him accordingly after a bishop who subscribed at the third Council of Paris in 557. Jacques du Perron, bishop of Angoulême, almoner to Queen Henrietta Maria, took this view of his predecessor, the almoner of Queen Bertha, that he had been Bishop of Senlis. The parallel which he drew between the two cases of the first Christian queen and her almoner, and the first Romanist queen after the final rupture and her almoner, was much in point. "Gaul it was that sent to the English their first Christian queen. The clergy of Gaul it was that sent them their first bishop, her almoner." But the sacramentary of Senlis, the calendar of commemorations, and the list of bishops, all are silent as to this Bishop Lethardus. Let me note for future use that these places, Soissons and Senlis, were in Belgic Gaul, that part of the continent which was directly opposite to the south-eastern parts of Britain.

I have said more about the diocese to which Luidhard may have belonged than I think the question deserves. This is done out of respect to my predecessors in the enquiry. The idea that a bishop must have had a see is natural enough to us, but is not according to knowledge. A hundred and fifty years later than this, there were so many wandering bishops in Gaul, that a synod held in this very diocese of Soissons declared that wandering bishops must not ordain priests; but that if any priests thus ordained were good priests, they should be reordained. And a great Council of all the bishops of Gaul, held at Verneuil in 755, declared that wandering bishops, who had not dioceses, should be incapable of performing any function without permission of the diocesan bishop. There is no suggestion that these were foreign bishops; and it was before the time when the invasions of Ireland by the Danes drove into England and on to the continent a perfect plague of Irish ecclesiastics calling themselves bishops. I think it is on the whole fair to say that the more you study the early history of episcopacy in these parts of Europe, the less need you feel to find a see for Bishop Luidhard.

There is one very interesting fact, which deserves to be noted in connection with this mysterious Gallican bishop. The Italian Mission paid very special honour to his memory and his remains. There is in the first volume of Dugdale's *Monasticon*[5] a copy of an ancient drawing of St. Augustine's, Canterbury. This is not, of course, the Cathedral Church, which was an old church of the British times restored by Augustine and dedicated to the Saviour; "Christ Church" it still remains. St. Augustine's was the church and monastery begun in Augustine's lifetime, and dedicated soon after his death to St. Peter and St. Paul, as Bede (i. 33) and various documents tell us precisely. This fact, that the church was dedicated to St. Peter and St. Paul, was represented last June, when "the renewal of the dedication of England to St. Mary and St. Peter" took place[6], by the statement that "the first great abbey church of Canterbury was dedicated to St. Peter." In the preparatory pastoral, signed by Cardinal Vaughan and fourteen other Roman Catholic Bishops, dated May 20, 1893, the statement took this form[7]:—"The second monastery of Canterbury was dedicated to St. Peter himself." Not only is that not so, but I cannot find evidence that Augustine dedicated any church anywhere "to St. Peter himself." Of the two Apostles, St. Peter and St. Paul, who were united in the earliest of all Saints' days, and still are so united in the Calendar of the Roman Church, though we have given to them two separate days, of the two, if we must choose one of them, St. Paul, not St. Peter, was made by Augustine the Apostle of England. To St. Paul was dedicated the first church in England dedicated to either of the two "himself," that is, alone; and that, too, this church, the first and cathedral church of the greater of the two places assigned by Gregory as the two Metropolitical sees of England, London and York.

The "dedication of England to St. Mary" has a similar difficulty to face. There is no evidence that Augustine assigned any dedication to the Blessed Virgin. The first church mentioned with that dedication was built by Laurentius and dedicated by Mellitus. But if twenty churches had been dedicated by Augustine to the Virgin and to St. Peter, England would have been the richer by twenty churches, and that would have been all.

The ancient drawing to which I am referring was made after 1325, when St. Ethelbert was added to the Apostles Peter and Paul and St. Augustine in the dedication of the high altar. It was copied for Sir William Dugdale's purposes in 1652, at which time it had passed into the safe hands of one of the Cambridge Colleges, Trinity Hall. The altar is shewn as deeply recessed into a structural reredos. A large number of shrines are shewn, ranged in semi-circles behind the reredos. On either side of the altar there is a door, as in our reredos at St. Paul's. They are marked "north door" and "south door," "to the bodies of the saints." On the shrines, shewn in the apse to which these doors lead, are written the names of those whose relics they contained, and the roll of names is illustrious. In the centre, at the extreme east, is Augustine, with

Laurentius and Mellitus north and south of him: then, on the north, Justus, Deusdedit, Mildred, Nothelm, and Lambert; on the south, Honorius, Theodore, Abbat Hadrian, Berhtwald, and Tatwin. Besides these shrines in the apse, behind the reredos, there is shewn immediately above the altar itself a prominent shrine, marked Scs. Ethelbertus, the relics of the first Christian king. Then, behind that, a number of books—manuscripts, of course—with a Latin description stating that they are "books sent by Gregory to Augustine"—one or two of which are still in existence. Above these, on either side of a great vesica enclosing a representation of our Lord, are two shrines, one marked "Relics," the other, which stands on the side of greater honour, is marked Scs. Letald(us). Thus the Canterbury monks at St. Augustine's, the great treasure-house of early Canterbury saints, put in the places of highest honour the relics of Bertha's husband and of Bertha's Gallican bishop. It is a pleasant thought in these days of ecclesiastical jealousies—and when were there days, before Christ or since, without ecclesiastical jealousies?—it is a very pleasant thought that the successors of Augustine paid such honour to Augustine's Gallican precursor, whose work they might almost have been expected, considering the temper of the times, to be inclined to ignore. The shrine with Luidhard's relics no doubt represents the golden chest in which—as we know—they used to carry his relics round Canterbury on Rogation Days.

It is not easy, indeed it is not possible, to make sure of the dates connected with Luidhard's work among the English at Canterbury—to give them the general name of "English." It is of some importance to make the attempt. The indications seem to me to point to a ministry of some considerable duration; but I am aware that among the many views expressed incidentally in the books, some names of great weight appear on the other side. When Ethelbert died in 616, Bede tells us that he had reigned gloriously for fifty-six years; that is, he began to reign in 560, a date earlier than that assigned by the Chronicle. Matthew of Westminster thinks Bede and the rest were wrong. With the Chronicle, he puts Ethelbert's accession later, as late as 566; but he keeps to Bede's fifty-six years' reign, and so makes him die in 622, much too late. If, as is said[8], he was born in 552, he was eight years old at his accession—rather an early age for an English sovereign in those times—and sixty-four at his death. His wife Bertha, whose marriage dates the arrival of Luidhard, was the daughter of Charibert, king of that part of the domains of his grandfather Clovis which gave to its sovereign the title of King of Paris. Her mother was Ingoberga; and if the statement of Gregory of Tours, that king Charibert married Ingoberga, is to be taken strictly, i.e. if he married her after his accession, Bertha was born about 561. But I much doubt whether Charibert had time for all his many marital wickednesses in his short reign, and I am inclined to think that he married a good deal earlier. He was the eldest son of his father Clotaire, who died in 561, and the known dates of Clovis make it probable that Charibert was of marriageable age a good many years before he succeeded his father.

So far as these considerations go, Bertha may have been of much the same age as her husband Ethelbert, and their marriage may have taken place about the year 575. I find nothing in the notices of Gregory of Tours inconsistent with this. Indeed, it may fairly be said that Gregory's facts indicate a date quite as early as that I have suggested. Ingoberga put herself under Gregory's own special charge. He describes her admirable manner of life in her widowhood, passed in a religious life, without any hint that her daughter was with her; and when she died in 589, Gregory guessed her age at seventy.

The chief reason for assigning a later date to the marriage is that King Edwin of Northumbria married Ethelberga, Bertha's daughter, in 625. Edwin was then a middle-aged widower, but that does not quite decide for us what sort of age he was likely to look for in a second wife. If Ethelberga was thirty when she married Edwin, Bertha would be about forty, or a little more, when her daughter was born.

There is one argument in favour of Bertha's marriage having been long before the coming of Augustine, which has, I think, generally escaped notice. In the letter which Gregory sent from Rome to Bertha, congratulating her on the conversion of her husband, Gregory urges her, now that, the time is fit, to repair what has been neglected; he remarks that she ought some time ago, or long ago, to have bent her husband's mind in this direction; and he tells her that the Romans have earnestly prayed for her life. All this, especially the "some time ago," or "long ago," looks unlike a recent marriage. It is interesting to notice, in view of recent assertions and claims, that Gregory does not make reference to St. Peter in this letter, as Boniface did in writing to Bertha's daughter. In his letter to Ethelbert, Gregory remarks at the end that he is sending him some small presents, which will not be small to him, as they come from the benediction of the blessed Peter the Apostle. Boniface, his fifth successor, considerably developed the Petrine position. Writing to Edwin of Northumbria, curiously enough while he was still a pagan, he says:—"We have sent to you a benediction of your protector the blessed Peter, prince of the Apostles, that is to say, a chemise embroidered with gold, and a garment of Ancyra." Probably Boniface did not know how nearly related the Galatian workers of the garment of Ancyra were to the Gallo-Britons whom Edwin's ancestors had expelled. And his letter to Ethelberga ended in the same way: —"We have sent to you a blessing of your protector the blessed Peter, prince of the Apostles, that is to say, a silver mirror and an ivory comb inlaid with gold." It is a significant note on this difference of language, that in the ordinary lists, where a distinction, more or less arbitrary, is made between bishops and popes, the break comes between Gregory and Boniface.

On the whole, then, I believe that Ethelbert and Bertha had been married many years when Augustine came, and, by consequence, that Luidhard had been living among the English many years. Though his work was in the end barren, there had been times when it was distinctly promising. His experiment had so far succeeded, that only more help was wanted to bring the heathen people to Christ. That help he had sought; perhaps especially when he felt old age coming upon him. Gregory distinctly states, in more than one of his letters, that the English people were very ready, were desirous, to be converted, and that applications for missionary help had been made, but made in vain, to the neighbouring priests. The tone and address of the letters imply that this meant the clergy of the neighbouring parts of Gaul. There certainly would be no response if they applied to the very nearest part they could reach by the ordinary route, namely, their landing-place, Boulogne. We Londoners are accustomed to say, no doubt with due contrition, but at the same time with some lurking sense of consequence, as having been actors in a striking episode, that after a few years of Christianity we went off into paganism again in a not undramatic manner, and from 616 to 654 repudiated Christianity. This fact is indicated by an eloquent void on our alabaster tablets of bishops of London in the south aisle of this church. At the time of which I am speaking, 594 or thereabouts, the Gauls of Boulogne were having the experience which the English of London were so soon to have. In London we turned out our first Italian bishop, our first bishop, that is, of the second series of bishops of London, after the restoration of Christianity on this site. In Boulogne and Terouenne, where the first bishop they ever had was sent to them after the year 500, they relapsed into paganism in about fifty years' time, and in 594 they had been pagans for many years. Pagans they remained till 630, when Dagobert got St. Omer to win them back. St. Omer died in 667, the year after Cedd died, who won us back. It is clear, then, that the appeals from the English to the Gauls for conversion, at any date consistent with the facts, must have gone beyond Boulogne.

It has been thought that the appeal was made to the British priests, who had retired to the mountainous parts of the island, beyond the reach of the slaying Saxon; but there would be no point in Gregory's remarks to his Gallican correspondents if that were so. And how Gregory was to know that appeals had been made by the English to the Britons for instruction in Christianity, appeals most improbable from the nature of the case, no one can say. On the other hand, he was distinctly in a position to know of such application to the Gauls, for his presbyter Candidus had gone to Gaul, and there was to purchase some pagan English boys of seventeen or eighteen to be brought up in monasteries. This had taken place a very short time before the mission set out, as is clear from Gregory's letter to the Patrician of Gaul.

The facts suggest that Luidhard was now quite an old man, and had failed to get any Gallican bishop to take up the work he could no longer carry on. And accordingly, tradition makes him die a month or two after Augustine's arrival. If we look to the language of Bede, we shall see, I think, that Luidhard had become incapable of carrying on his work when Augustine and his companions arrived. For they at once entered upon the use of his church. "There was on the east side of the city a church erected of old in honour of St. Martin[9], when the Romans were still inhabiting Britain, where the queen used to pray. In this church they met at first, to sing, pray, celebrate masses, preach, and baptise; till the king, on his conversion, gave them larger licence, to preach anywhere, and to build and restore churches."

Now, quite apart from Luidhard's long and faithful work, we have seen that there was in Canterbury the fabric of a Christian church remaining from the time before the English came; and that there was in Canterbury the fabric of another church, out of which they made their Cathedral church.

There was a church in existence at Canterbury when our bishop Mellitus was archbishop there, between 619 and 624, dedicated to the Four Crowned Martyrs of Diocletian's persecution, the Quattro Santi Incoronati, whose church is one of the most interesting in Rome. But this Canterbury church may have been built by the Italians.

Again, there is very unmistakable and interesting Roman work at St. Pancras, in Canterbury; and this was, according to tradition, the temple which Ethelbert had appropriated for the worship of his idols, and now gave for Christian purposes. The tradition further says that it had once been a Christian church, before the pagan English came; and the remains of the Roman building still visible are believed to point in that direction. The church of St. Pancras at Rome was built about 500. In connection with this idea of a pagan temple being used by the Christian clergy for a church, we may remember that the Pantheon at Rome was turned into a church seven or eight years after this, the dedication being changed from "all the Gods" to "St. Mary of the Martyrs," and this was the origin of the Festival of All Saints[10]. Bede adds an important fact, that Ethelbert gave the Italians a general licence to restore churches.

How did it come about that when the Italians came to heathen England, they found here these remains of Christian churches, needing only repair? Who built them? Was it an accidental colony of Christians, that had been settled in Canterbury, or had there been what we may call a British Church, a Christian church in Britain, long before the Saxons came, longer still by far before the Italians? The answer to those questions is not a short or a simple one, when we once get beyond the bare "yes" and "no." Many other questions rise up on all sides, when we are looking for an answer to the original questions. It is my aim to take those who care to come with me over some parts of the field of inquiry; rather courting than avoiding incidental illustrations and digressions; for I think that in that informal way we pick up a good deal of interesting information, and get perhaps to feel more at home in a period than by pursuing a more formal and stilted course. Indeed a good deal of what I have said already has evidently been said with that object.

The first question I propose for our consideration is this:—Who were the people who built the churches? It is not a very explanatory answer, to say "The Britons." There is a good deal left to the imagination in that answer, with most of us. With the help of the best qualified students, but without any hope that we could harmonise all the diverse views if we went far into detail, let us look into the matter a little. It may be well for all of us to remember in this enquiry that our foundations are not very solid; we are on thin ice. Nor is the way very smooth; it is easy to trip.

We need not go back to the time of the cavemen, interesting and indeed artistic as the evidence of their remains shews them to have been. Their reign was over before Britain became an island, before a channel separated it from the continent. It is enough for our present purpose to realise, that when the great geological changes had taken place which produced something like the present geographical arrangements, but still in prehistoric times, times long before the beginning of history so far as these islands are concerned, our islands were occupied by a race which existed also in the north-west and extreme west of Europe. Herodotus knew nothing of the existence of our islands; but he tells us that in his time the people furthest to the west, nearer to the setting sun than even the Celtae, were called Kynesii, or Kynetes. Archaeological investigations shew that, though he did not know it, his statement covered our islands. The people of whom he wrote were certainly here as well as on the western parts of the continent. As some of us may have some of their blood in our veins, we may leave others to discuss the question whether the names Kynesii, Kynetes, mean "dog-men," and if so, what that implies. St. Jerome in the course of his travels, say about 370 years after Christ, saw a body of savage soldiers in the Roman army, brought from a part of what is now Scotland—if an Englishman dare say such a thing; they were fed, he tells us, on human flesh. The locality from which they came indicates that they were possibly representatives of these earlier "dog-men," if that is the meaning of Kynetes. Secular historians, long before Jerome, have an uncomfortable way of saying that the inhabitants of the interior of Britain were cannibals, and their matrimonial arrangements resembled those of herds of cattle. As we in London had relations with the centre of the country, we may argue—and I think rightly—that by "the interior" the historians did not mean what we call the Midlands, but meant the parts furthest removed from the ports of access in the south-east, that is, the far west and the far north.

Next, and again before the history of our islands begins, an immigration of Celts[11] took place, a people belonging—unlike the earlier race of whom I have spoken—to the same Indo-European family of nations to which the Latins, and the Teutons, and the Greeks, and the speakers of Sanskrit, belonged. Of their various cousin-nations, these Celts were nearest in language to the Latins, we are told, and, after the Latins, to the Teutons. They came to this island, it is understood, from the country which we call France.

Thirdly, the Gauls, who on the continent had both that name and the name of the older Celts[12], and must be regarded as the dominant sub-division of their race, impelled in their turn by pressure from the south and east, came over into these islands, and here were called Britons[13]. They squeezed out the earlier occupants from most part of the larger island, driving them north and west and south-west, as the Celtic inhabitants long before had driven the earlier race. When the Romans came, fifty years before Christ, these Britons occupied the land practically from the south coast to the further side of the Firth of Forth. There had been for some time before Caesar's arrival a steady inflow of Belgic Gauls, people from the eastward parts of what we call France; and these people, the most recent comers among the Britons, were found chiefly on the coasts, but in parts had extended to considerable distances inland. The Celts, to distinguish the preceding immigrants by that name, though in fact it does not properly convey the distinction, occupied Devon and Cornwall, South Wales, the north-west corner of North Wales, Cumberland, and the south-west of what we now call Scotland, that is, Wigton, Kirkcudbright, Dumfries, and part of Ayr. They occupied also a belt of Caledonia north of Stirling. They occupied at least the eastern parts of Ireland. Anglesey and Man were in their hands. The parts of Scotland north of Perthshire and Forfar may be regarded as the principal refuge of the remnant of the people whom we have described as the earlier race, before the Celts; and there were traces of them left in almost all the parts occupied by their immediate successors the Celts. The name by which we ought probably to call these latter, the Celts, in whatever part of the islands they might be, has been familiarly used in a sense so limited that it might cause confusion to use it now in its larger sense. I mean Gael, and Gaelic.

Now we gather from the records that before the Jutes and the Angles and the Saxons came, and in their turn drove the Britons north and west, the religion of Christ had spread to all parts of the territory occupied by the Britons, that is, to the towns in all parts. It may very well have been that in the country parts there were many pagans left even to the last, perhaps in towns too. Putting the commencement of the driving out of the Britons at about the year 450 after Christ, we know that less than a hundred years before that time the pagans were so numerous in Gaul, that when Martin became Bishop of Tours, the pagans were everywhere, and to work for their conversion would have been sufficient work for him. As for the towns in Gaul, Hilary, the Bishop of Poitiers, was a leading official in that town, and only became a Christian in the year 350, when he was about thirty-five years of age. Martin of Tours, too, was born a heathen. We may be sure that in Britain, so remote from the centres of influence, and so inaccessible by reason of its insular position, that state of things continued to prevail a good deal longer than in the civilised parts of Gaul. We must not credit our British predecessors with anything like a universal knowledge and acceptance of Christianity.

It is not necessary to dwell on the familiar fact of the intermixture of the Romans and the Britons. In the more important towns there was much blending of the two races, and the luxurious arts of Rome produced their effect in softening the British spirit. The Briton gave up more than he gained in the mixed marriages, and it seems clear that the Romano-Britons who were left to face the barbarous Picts and Scots, and the hardy Angles and Saxons, were by comparison an enervated race. In the parts further remote from commercial and municipal centres, and from the military lines, it is probable that the invaders found much tougher work. It is only fair to the later Romano-Britons, to remember that all the flower of the youth of Britain had been carried away by one general and emperor after another, to fight the battles of Rome, or to support the claims of a usurper of the imperial purple, in Gaul and Spain and Italy; and when the imperial troops were finally withdrawn, the older men and the less hardy of the youths of Britain were left to cope with enemies who had baffled the Roman arms.

So much for the Britons. As for the Celts, we have sufficient evidence that the message of Christ was taken to them and welcomed by them in the later parts of the period ending with 450. During the years of the struggle between the Britons and their Teutonic invaders, say from 450 to 590, this Christianising went on among the Celts. About the end of that period it reached even to the furthest parts of the north, the parts which, in the early times of the Roman occupation, were probably held by descendants of the earlier race, and it more or less covered Ireland.

Thus the knowledge of the Christian faith had, before the English came, extended over the whole of that part of this island which the English invaders in their furthest reach ever occupied. It had covered—and it continued to cover, and has never ceased to cover—very much that they never even touched. To convert the early English to Christ, which was the task undertaken by Augustine, a very small part of it being accomplished by him or his mission from first to last, was to restore Christianity to those parts from which the English had driven it out. It was to remove the barrier of heathendom which the English invaders had formed between the Church universal and the Celtic and British church or churches. It proved in the end that the undertaking was much beyond the powers of the Italian missionaries; and then the earlier church stepped in from its confines in the West and did the work. It was so that the great English province of Northumbria—meaning vastly more than Northumberland, even all the land from Humber to Forth—was evangelized. It was so that the great English province of Mercia—the whole of the middle of the island—received the message of Christ. It was so that Christianity was given back to Essex and to us in London, by the labours of our Bishop Cedd, consecrated, as the crown of his long and faithful labours among our heathen predecessors, by the Celtic Bishop Finan of Lindisfarne. Cedd is an admirable example of the careful methods of the Celtic Church. He was not a Celt himself, he was an Angle. When the English branch of the Celtic Church, settled at Lindisfarne and evangelizing Northumbria, had succeeded in converting the son of the Mercian king, they sent him four priests as missionaries to his people, a people who were in large part Angles. Of these four priests, trained and sent by the Celtic Church for the conversion of the English, only one was a Celt; the other three, including Cedd, were themselves Angles. To send Anglian priests to convert Anglian people was indeed a wise and broad policy; and it was, as it deserved to be, eminently successful. It is a striking contradiction of the prevalent idea that the Celtic Church was isolated, narrow, bigoted; unable and unwilling to work with any but those of its own blood.

There are, then, these two main divisions before us, of the people who occupied these islands when the Romans came, and still occupied them when the English came, the Britons and the Celts[14]. We are not to suppose that this is nothing more than a mere dead piece of archaeology. It is a very living fact. A large proportion of those who are here to-day have to-day—possibly some of them not knowing it—kept alive the distinction between Briton and Celt. Every one who has spoken the name Mackenzie, or Macpherson, or any other Mac, has used the Celtic speech in its most characteristic feature. Every one who has spoken the name Price, that is, ap Rhys, or any other name formed with ap[15], has taken the Briton's side on this characteristic point. When you speak of Pen(maen)maur and the king Malcolm Ceanmor you are saying the same words; but in Penmaenmaur you take the Briton's side, in speaking of

Ceanmor you take the Celt's. You will not find a better example than that which we owe to our dear Bede. The wall of Antonine abuts on the river Forth at Kinnell, a name which does not seem to have much to do with the end of a wall. But Bede tells us that the Picts of his day called it Penfahel, that is, head of the wall, "fahel" being only "wall" pronounced as some of our northern neighbours would pronounce it, the interesting people who say "fat" for "what." He adds that the English, his own people, called it Penel, cutting the Penfahel short. The Britons called it Penguaul. The modern name Kinnell is the Celtic form of Penel.

Those being the people, and that the extent to which Christianity had in the end spread among them, how did Christianity find its way here?

The various suggestions that have from time to time been made, in the course of the early centuries, as to the introduction of Christianity to this island, were collected and commented on in a searching manner twenty-five years ago by two men of great learning and judgement. One of them was taken away from historical investigations, and from his canonry of St. Paul's, to the laborious and absorbing work of a bishop. The other was lost to historical study by death. I need scarcely name Dr. Stubbs and Mr. Haddan. Their work has made darkness almost light.

We cannot wonder that the marvellous apostolic journeys and missionary work of St. Paul so vividly impressed the minds of the early Christian writers, that they attributed to him even more than he actually performed. Clement of Rome, of whom I suppose the great majority of students of the Scripture and of Church History believe that he actually knew St. Paul, says that Paul preached both in the West and in the East, and taught the whole world, even to the limits of the West. Chrysostom says that from Illyricum Paul went to the very ends of the earth. These are the strongest statements which can be advanced by those who think that St. Paul himself may have visited Britain. He may have reached Spain. There does not appear to be any evidence that he ever reached Gaul; still less Britain. One of the Greek historians, Eusebius, writing about 315, appears to say that Britain was Christianised by some of the disciples; and another, Theodoret, about 423, names the Britons among those who were persuaded to receive the laws of the Crucified, by "our fishermen and publicans." This is evidence, and very interesting evidence, of the general belief that Britain was Christianised early in the history of Christianity, but it practically amounts to nothing more definite than that[16].

But a very curious connection may be made out, between the Britons and the great apostle of the Gentiles.

In speaking of the relations, real or fairly imaginable, between Soissons or Senlis and the English in the parts of the island which lie opposite to that part of Gaul, I asked you to note that this was Belgic Gaul. We have seen that for some time before Julius Caesar's invasion a change had been going on in the population of those parts of Britain to which I now refer. The Belgae had been crossing the narrow sea and settling here, presumably driving away the inhabitants whom they found. They so specially occupied the parts where now Hampshire is, that the capital city, Went, was named from them by the Latins Venta Belgarum, Belgian Venta; to return in later times to its old name of Caer Went, this is, Went Castle, Winchester. Indeed, the Belgae are credited with the occupation of territory up to the borders of Devon. The British tribe of the Atrebates, again, were the same people as the Gauls in the district of Arras; and they occupied a large tract of country stretching away from the immediate west of London. Caesar remarks on this fact that the immigrant Gauls retained the names of their continental districts and cities. The Parisii on the east coast, north of the Humber, afford another illustration.

Now when Jerome, about the year 367, was at Trèves, the capital of Gaul, situate in Belgic Gaul, he learned the native tongue of the Belgic Gauls; and when later in his life he travelled through Galatia, in Asia Minor, he found the people there speaking practically the same language as the Gauls about Trèves. Thus we are entitled to claim the Galatians as of kin to the Belgic division of the Gauls, and therefore as the same people with those who from before Caesar's time flowed steadily over from Belgic Gaul to Britain. That the Galatians were Gauls is of course a well-known fact in history; the point I wish to note is that they were Belgic Gauls. We may therefore see in St. Paul's epistle to the Galatian churches a description of the national character of the Britons of these parts of the island. Fickleness, superstition, and quarrelsomeness, are the characteristics on which he remarks. The very first words of the Epistle, after the preface, strike a clear and forcible note:—"I marvel that ye are so quickly moved to abandon the gospel of him that called you, for another gospel." Again, "O foolish Galatians, who hath bewitched you!" "Ye were in bondage to them which are by nature no gods;… how turn ye back again to the weak and beggarly rudiments, whereunto ye desire to be in bondage over again!" "If ye bite and devour one another." Without at all saying that these national characteristics are traceable in any parts of our islands now, it is evident that they are in close accord with what we hear of the early inhabitants. As also is another remark made in early times, "the Gauls begin their fights with more than the strength of men, they finish them with less than the strength of women."

The line taken by a recent writer, Professor W. M. Ramsay, in his most interesting and able book, "The Church in the Roman Empire," traverses this argument about the Galatian Epistle. In opposition to the great divine who for eight years spoke from this pulpit, and made this Epistle a special study for a great part of his life, Professor Ramsay maintains, by arguments drawn from geographical and epigraphical facts not known thirty years ago, when Dr. Lightfoot first wrote, that the Epistle was addressed to the people in the southern part of the Roman province called Galatia, who were not Galatians at all; and was not addressed to those in the northern part, who were Galatians proper, and occupied the whole of the country named from them Galatia. But I use the illustration, notwithstanding this. The controversy is not quite ended yet; and I do not feel sure that the difficulties of the Epistle itself, from Professor Ramsay's point of view, are very much less considerable than those which Dr. Lightfoot's view undoubtedly has to face. In any case the Galatians proper were of close kin with the more civilised of our British predecessors—ancestors we may perhaps say—and this at least gives us a personal interest in what at first sight would seem to be a very far-off controversy.

The tradition which used to find most favour was that Joseph of Arimathea came over with twelve companions, and received from a British king in the south-west a portion of land for each of his companions, and founded the ecclesiastical establishment of Glastonbury. There is certainly some very ancient history connected with the "twelve hides" of Glastonbury. Go as far back as we will in the records, we never come to the beginning of the "xii. hidæ." The Domesday Survey tells us, eight hundred years ago, that the twelve hides "never have been taxed." Clearly they take us back to some very early donation; and I see no reason—beyond the obvious difficulty of its geographical remoteness—against the tradition that here was the earliest Christian establishment in Britain. At the Council of Basle, in 1431, when the Western Church was holding councils with a view to reforming from within the enormous abuses of the Roman Court, a prelude to the "Reformation" into which we were driven a hundred years later, the precedence of churches was determined by the date of their foundation. The English Church claimed and received precedence as founded in Apostolic times by Joseph of Arimathea. Those were not very critical days, so far as historical evidence was concerned, and I should not have mentioned this legend, or should only have mentioned it and passed on, but for a recent illustration of a part of the story. The more we look into early local legends, the more disinclined we become to say that there is nothing substantial in them. The story has from early times gone, that the first British Christians erected at Glastonbury a church made of twigs, of wattle-work. This wattle church survived the violent changes which swept over the face of the land. Indeed, it is said, and with so much of probability that Mr. Freeman was willing to accept it as a fact, that Glastonbury was the one place outside the fastnesses to which the British Christians fled, where Christian worship was not interrupted when the English came. This wattle church survived till after the Norman invasion, when it was burned by accident[17]. Wattle-work is a very perishable material; and of all things of the kind the least likely would seem to be, that we, in this nineteenth century, should, in confirmation of the story, discover at Glastonbury an almost endless amount of British wattle-work. Yet that is exactly what has happened. In the low ground, now occupying the place of the impenetrable marshes which gave the name of the Isle of Avalon to the higher ground, the eye of a local antiquary had long marked a mass of dome-shaped hillocks, some of them of very considerable diameter, and about seventy in number, clustered together in what is now a large field, a mile and a quarter from Glastonbury. The year before last he began to dig. Peat had formed itself in the long course of time, and its preservative qualities had kept safe for our eyes that which it enclosed and covered. The hillocks proved to be the remains of British houses burned with fire. They were set on ground made solid in the midst of waters, with causeways for approach from the land. The faces of the solid ground and the sides of the causeways are revetted with wattle-work. There is wattle-work all over, strong and very well made. It clearly was the main stand-by of the Britons, whose fortress this was, and their skill in making it and applying it was great. The wattle when first uncovered is as good to all appearance as the day it was made. The huts are oval and circular, and some are of large dimensions. The largest of all are not yet opened, but already a hut covering about 450 square feet has been found. All have a circular area of white stones in the middle, carried from far, for a hearth, &c., and all have been destroyed by fire. But though the fire has destroyed the huts completely, it has preserved for us the account of the material of which they were made, as clearly as if it were inscribed on the brick cylinders of an Assyrian king. It has baked the clay with which the huts were covered, and the baked clay shews the impress of wattle-work. The houses of the Britons at Glastonbury were, as a matter of fact, as long tradition tells us their church was, made of wattles[18].

Julius Caesar speaks more than once of the skill of the British in this respect. He tells us of the plaiting together of the branches of growing trees to form barriers in the woods, which his soldiers found unpleasantly effective. We read also of the wattle-work erections of various shapes in which human victims were enclosed to be burned. And, from a more peaceful side, we learn that the tables of ladies in Rome were not completely in the fashion if they had no examples of British baskets. "Basket," as you know, is one of the best examples of the survival of a British word among us, a word used also by the Romans[19], their word *bascauda* and our "basket" representing the Welsh *basgawd* and *basget*.

There is abundance of evidence of the interest taken by the Romans in Britain and its people, and of the esteem in which Britons were held at Rome. Martial, who settled in Rome in the year A. D. 66, perhaps one year or two years before St. Paul's death, speaks of a British lady in Rome, Claudia, the newly-married wife of Pudens. Of her he says[20], in terms as he believed of the highest personal praise—

> Though Claudia from the sea-green Britons came,
> She wears the aspect of a Roman dame.

And, again, he mentions, not without pride, that he was read in Britain: 'Britain, too, is said to sing my verse.' It is a little difficult to resist the tendency to see in this Pudens and Claudia the Pudens and Claudia of the last sentence before the final blessing in the last letter of St. Paul, where their names are linked together by that of Linus, the first Bishop of Rome. We are told, however, that the severe historian ought to resist this tendency of the natural man.

Again, Seneca, the brother of Gallio, whom we meet in the Acts, had a great deal of money invested in Britain. Juvenal brings a British king into his verse, and Richborough oysters. Josephus[21] tells us that Titus made use of the Britons, as a telling illustration in his final speech to the desperate Jews: —"Pray what greater obstacle is there than the wall of the Ocean, with which the Britons are encompassed? And yet they bow before the arms of the Romans."

Those are probably sufficient indications of the kind of evidence we have. We know, too, that the Roman troops came and went; and we may be sure that they made Britain and the strange things they had seen here a frequent subject of conversation. We cannot doubt that St. Paul, in his enforced intercourse with the soldiery at Rome, learned all he could about the distant parts of the world, which only the Roman armies had visited. Nay, we in London may go further than that. Seeing that Nero recalled from Britain the victorious Suetonius in 61, and that St. Paul lived with Roman soldiers in all probability from 61 to 63, we may imagine that some soldier or other described to St. Paul that terrible day on which Suetonius made up his mind that he must leave London to its fate. You remember the account of Tacitus[22], so telling in its studied brevity. It is, I think, the first definite appearance of London on the stage of history. The occasion was the revolt of Boadicea, to retain the familiar incorrectness of the name. Colchester had fallen, all the Romans there being slaughtered. The ninth legion had been attacked and routed by the Britons, and all the infantry killed. Many a gallant fight no doubt in the thick woods, like that which Wilson and his comrades fought last month[23]. The governor of the province fled to Gaul. Verulam fell, with great slaughter. There was no taking captive, no selling into slavery. The Britons made sure work; they burned, they tortured, they crucified. One man of the Romans kept his head, or all would have been massacred. With a constancy which made men marvel, Suetonius marched through the midst of foes to the relief of London—London not then illustrious as a colony, but more famous than any other city in the land for the number of its merchants and the abundance of its merchandise. Should he make London his centre of defence? He looked at the small number of his soldiers: he thought of the destruction of the ninth legion. He determined to leave London to its fate. Tears and prayers could not move him. He gave the signal to march. Those of the citizens who accompanied him his soldiers protected. All who remained behind, unable or unwilling to leave their homes, all were overwhelmed in one great slaughter. The Romans calculated that at Colchester, Verulam, and London, from seventy to eighty thousand of Romans and their allies were slain by the enraged Britons[24]. We may imagine how St. Paul would listen to that tale of woe, then quite fresh, the most tragic event of the time; and how he would long for an opportunity of softening the disposition of the Britons by the gentle doctrines of Christ.

To no such source as that, however, are we to look for the beginnings of the faith among us. There is no sign of any one great effort, by any one great man, to introduce Christianity into our land. It came, we cannot doubt, in the natural way, simply and quietly, through the nearest continental neighbours of the Britons and their nearest kinsfolk, the people of Gaul. That will form the main subject of my next lecture.

LECTURE II.

> Early mentions of Christianity in Britain.—King Lucius.—Origin and spread of Christianity in Gaul.—British Bishops at Councils.—Pelagianism.—British Bishops of London.—Fastidius.

We are to consider this evening the Christian Church in Britain, from the earliest times at which we have any definite notice of it, to the time of its expulsion from what had become England. It may be well to take notice first of one or two statements of early writers about the existence of Christianity here, at dates precisely known.

Tertullian, writing in or about the year 208, at a time when a revolt against Severus in the north of this island gave special point to his remark, thus describes the wide spread of the Gospel. "In all parts of Spain, among the various nations of Gaul, in districts of Britain inaccessible to the Romans but subdued to Christ, in all these the kingdom and name of Christ are venerated." Origen, in 239, speaking of polytheism, asks, "When, before the coming of Christ, did the land of Britain hold the belief in the one God?" And again:—"The power of the Saviour is felt even among those who are divided from our world, in Britain." At the same time Origen gives us a timely warning against taking his remarks to mean anything like the complete Christianisation of the island; he tells us that among the Britons, and six other nations whom he names, "very many have not yet heard the word of the Gospel."

The Greek historian Sozomen speaks of Constantine living in Gaul and Britain, and there, as, he says, was universally admitted, becoming a Christian. Both Eusebius, writing about 320, and Sozomen, about 443, tell of an experiment made in the palace by Constantine's father Constantius, when he governed Gaul and Britain, which shews the spread of the gospel and the high places it had by that time reached. It has this special interest for Britain, that York was one of the two cities at one of which it must have taken place, Trèves being the other; for those were the two capitals and seats of government of the whole province of the Gauls, the one for the continental the other for the insular department of the province. A persecution of the Christians was ordered by his three colleagues in the empire, about the year 303. Constantius, though not himself a Christian, did not allow much severity in his own government; a contemporary writer, Lactantius, declares that from east to west three savage beasts raged; everywhere but in the Gauls, that is, Gaul and Britain. The experiment was this. He told the officers of his court, who are spoken of as if all were Christians, though he himself was not, that those of them who would sacrifice to demons should remain with him and enjoy their honours: those who would not, should be banished from his presence. He gave them time to think the matter over. They came to him again, each with his mind made up; and some said they would sacrifice, and some said they would not. When all had declared their intention, he told those who would sacrifice, that if they were ready to be false to their God, he did not see how he could trust them to be true to him. To the others he said that such worthy servants of their God would be faithful to their king too. The story reminds us of the sturdy old pagan king of Mercia, Penda, who said he was quite willing that the Lindisfarne missionaries should convert his people to Christianity, if they could; but he gave full warning that he would not have people calling themselves Christians and not living up to their high profession.

This story of Constantius, the father of Constantine, which I prefer to place at York, the favourite residence of Constantius, introduces us of course to the one well-known result of the persecution, so far as Britain was concerned, the death of Alban at Verulam, about 305. When you go to St. Albans, you see the local truth of the traditional details. Standing on the narrow bridge across the little stream, you realise the blocking of the bridge by the crowd of spectators nearly 1,600 years ago: and you can see Alban, in his eagerness to win his martyr's crown, pushing his way through the shallow water, rather than be delayed by the crowd on the bridge. There is an interesting coincidence, in connection with the story of St. Alban, which I have not seen noticed. The Gauls of Galatia, as we have seen, were of kin to the Britons; and while the Britons were being almost entirely saved from harm by Constantius, their Galatian cousins were passing through a very fiery trial. The persecution of Diocletian raged furiously in Galatia. As St. Alban is, I believe, the earliest example of a name attached to a Christian site in this island, so the earliest existing church in Ancyra, the capital of Gaulish Galatia, owes its name to St. Clement, the martyr bishop of Ancyra, St. Alban's contemporary in martyrdom.

It is unnecessary to say more on the evidence of Christianity in our island at least from 200 onwards. But, as I have said before, there is an entire dearth of information as to any special introduction of the new faith. It came. It grew. How it came; who planted it; who watered it; all is blank.

You are, of course, familiar with the story that Lucius, a British king, requested Eleutherus, or Eleutherius, Bishop of Rome 171 to 185, to send some one to teach his people Christianity, of which he had himself some knowledge. The documents which profess to be the letters connected with this request are unskilful forgeries. A note is appended to the name of Eleutherus in the *Catalogue of Roman Pontiffs* to the effect that "he received a letter from Lucius, a British king, requesting that he might be made a Christian." But this is a later addition, for it does not exist in the earlier catalogue, which was itself written nearly 200 years after the supposed event. It is an addition of the kind of which we have, alas! so many examples at Rome and elsewhere, but especially and above all at Rome: a statement inserted in later times for the sake of magnifying the claims to ecclesiastical authority, and affording evidence, in an uncritical age, of their recognition by former generations. The credit of this fallacious insertion has rather unkindly, but perhaps not unjustly, been assigned to Prosper of Aquitaine, of whom we shall hear again[25]. It is quite in his style.

It is natural to say, and many of us no doubt have said it, that there is no improbability in the statement that such an application was made. I used to think so, but each further investigation makes the improbability seem more real. Neither if we look to the Church of Rome, at the time, nor if we look to the state of Gaul, shall we find encouragement for a story, which in itself it would be very pleasant to believe of our British predecessors. It might be thought not unlikely that some Christian, escaping from the terrible persecutions just then enacted at Lyons and Vienne, had fled northwards through lands all pagan, and had reached pagan Britain. But if that were so, he would scarcely tell Lucius to send to Rome. There were Christians in Southern Gaul: send to them. The man's allegiance to a centre would be to Asia Minor, not to Rome. The Bishops of Rome, too, were not particularly strong men in early times, nor men of much distinction. The really great men were in the East; were in Africa; anywhere but Rome. The secular world was still ruled from the pagan city of Rome; but ecclesiastical Rome was not in a large way as yet: it did not as yet live up to its natural position. Rome was marked out by its supreme secular position to be the centre of the Western Church; and it had, besides, the great ecclesiastical claim of its origin. It was the most ancient of the Churches of the West. It alone could stand the test, stated so convincingly by Tertullian, of Apostolical foundation; for it, and it alone in the West, had a letter that could be read in its churches from the Apostle who founded it. Rome, as Tertullian says, had a letter written by its founder, equal in this supreme respect, as he puts it, to Corinth, Philippi, Thessalonica, Ephesus. It had also the exceptional happiness, as Tertullian justly describes it, of being the scene of the martyrdom of its founder, St. Paul; and of that other great Apostle who found a grave there, St. Peter; to which Tertullian adds the miracle of St. John at the Latin gate. The force of the claim which its secular position gave to it was fully and justly recognised by the Second General Council, in terms which are a permanent stumbling-block to the mediaeval claims of Rome. The Fathers, assembled in 381, declared that the see of Constantinople should rank next in precedence to the see of Rome, on the ground that Constantinople, now the seat of empire, was 'new Rome;' taking ecclesiastical rank from its secular position, as Rome itself had done. In the early times of which we are now speaking, we do not find even the germ of the mediaeval theory of Roman supremacy; and the men who filled the office of Bishop of Rome were not men of mark enough to work any approach to such a theory, or to fix upon them the eyes of a far-off barbarian chief. It was either this Eleutherus, or his successor Victor, who was all but taken in to recognise Montanism, as indeed Zosimus was taken in, 250 years later, by the superior subtlety of our countryman, the Briton Pelagius. Eleutherus, or Victor, was only saved from this grave mistake by the advice of an Oriental heretic.

But apart from all such considerations, which I mention historically and not polemically, I see no reason why Britons should go so far afield if they wished to learn of Christ. With Gaul so close at hand, its people so near of kin, its government so identical with theirs, the Britons would hear of Christianity, would learn Christianity, from and through Gaul, and would look to Gaul, not Italy. But if we look to the state of Gaul in the time to which this British king is assigned, we shall see that it was in the very highest degree improbable that he should aim at making his people Christians. It was a time of terrible trial, with everything to be lost by becoming Christian. What sort of Christian hero was this, in the year 175 or 180, who desired to lead his nation to a change in their religion, that they might court the barbarous tortures inflicted by their kinsfolk on all of the Christian name at this exact conjuncture?

The new faith was planted in the south of Gaul comparatively early, but it spread northwards very slowly. The first congregations, those of Lyons and Vienne, were formed by Christians from Asia Minor, where some of them had known Polycarp, who was a pupil of St. John. Soon after the foundation of this infant Church, the great persecution of its members took place, about the year 175, when Eleutherus was bishop of Rome. The details of the persecution are so well known, through the letter which the survivors wrote— not to Rome, but to their parent Church and personal friends in Asia and Phrygia,—a letter preserved to us by the Greek historian Eusebius, that I think they have given a wrong impression as to the extent of the Christian Church in Gaul towards the end of the second century[26]. The Christians at Lyons and Vienne were a small and isolated flock, not however isolated as foreigners speaking a strange tongue, for Irenaeus, who was one of them, mentions his daily use of the Gallic language. They seem to have been almost the only Christians known in Gaul. The ignorance of the practices of Christianity was so great among the Gauls, that they were accused of crimes such as they did not believe any man committed,—banquets of Thyestes, incests of Oedipus. That was in the year 175. Lyons was a wonderful water-centre. An examination of a good map will surprise even those who know France fairly well. North, south, east, and west, there were water-ways. Even Eusebius, writing far away in the East, remarked on this; and you know how tantalisingly silent early historians are as a rule about such things. And yet Christianity spread exceedingly slowly. Gregory of Tours, whose inclination would not be to make little of the early Church in Gaul, seeing that he was a Gallo-Roman of lofty lineage, and not a newfangled Frank, quotes with complete assent the statement that a great missionary effort had to be made in Gaul about the year 250 to spread Christianity; and that so late as that, missionary bishops had to be sent—neither he nor his authority says by whom —to seven cities and districts, in most of which, we should otherwise have supposed, Christianity in its full form had for many years existed. These were Tours, Arles, Narbonne, Toulouse, Paris, Auvergne, and Limoges[27]. With the exception of Paris, that does not carry us very far towards Britain, even in the middle of the third century. There is not any evidence, and without evidence it would be unreasonable to imagine so improbable a thing, that far-away Britain was in advance of Gaul by decades of Christian years. Gregory of Tours, however, was not completely informed. We may probably accept, as having some historical foundation, the story that some of those who escaped from the persecution at Lyons did push up northwards and teach Christianity at Autun, Dijon, and Langres. The last-named town was well up on one of the routes to Britain. It was the death-place of Abbot Ceolfrid on his journey towards Rome in 716.

If we look to the traditional dates of the establishment of bishoprics in the parts of Gaul which face the Britannic isles, we shall find that even tradition does not assign to them any very early origin. Beginning with the archdiocese of Rouen, and bearing in mind that it is not the way of ecclesiastical traditions to err on the side of lateness, the first dated bishops in the several dioceses are as follows. The third bishop of Rouen, or, as some count, the second, was at Arles in 314. The third bishop of Bayeux dates 458-65. The second bishop of Avranches, 511. The second bishop of Evreux, 450-90. The fifth bishop of Séez, 500. The first bishop of Lisieux whose name is recorded, 538. The first bishop of Coutances, about 475. As three British bishops were at Arles in 314, when only one of these seven bishoprics was in existence, the antiquity and completeness of our island Church compares very favourably with that of the archdiocese of Rouen. Passing to the archdiocese of Cambray, the first bishop of Cambray died in 540; the first bishop of Tournay is dated 297; the other bishoprics are late. In the archdiocese of Rheims, the two first bishops of Rheims, paired together, are assigned to 290; the two first bishops of Soissons were the same pair as those of Rheims; the first bishop of Lâon was at Orleans in 549; Beauvais, 250; Châlons about 280; the second bishop of Amiens, 346; the ninth of Senlis, 511; the second of Boulogne, 552. Here, again, our three bishops at Arles in 314 compare favourably with this great archdiocese, which was in the most accessible part of Gaul for the insular Britons.

Unless we are prepared to believe that our island was Christianised by some influence apart from Gaul, and reaching us through some route other than that of Gaul—and I do not see any evidence for anything of the kind—we must, I think, take it that our position was that of younger sister to the Church in Gaul. All the indications point in that direction. It is most cruel that the British history has all been blotted out, by the severity of the English conquest and the barbarity of the bordering tribes. In Gaul, the history was not blotted out by the successful invasion of the Franks. Gregory of Tours died in the year 594, of which we have said so much. He was a Gallo-Roman, one of the race overrun by the Franks; and yet he writes the history of the Franks, putting on record an immense amount of information about the earlier Gaulish times—not very trustworthy, it is true. But for the sack of London by the East Saxons, of which I shall have to speak later, we might have had a history that would solve all our doubts, from a Brito-Roman Bishop of London, exactly contemporary with Gregory of Tours. Failing all such record, we must read the signs for ourselves, and they point in the direction I have described. They make us a younger sister, not very much younger, of the Church of Gaul—a Church founded from Ephesus—Oriental in its origin, not Western. I may, perhaps, have time to indicate in my concluding lecture some points which shew the non-Western connection of the British Church.

The probability is that from Tertullian's time onwards the faith spread and grew here quietly. The Christian Church certainly took to itself an outward form. Bishops were appointed in central places. By the year 314—that is, in one century of growth—it appears that we had in Britain a Christian Church as fully equipped as any corresponding area of the Continent at that time was. What is the evidence for this?

At the Council of Arles, A. D. 314, three British bishops were present. Two of them are described as of the province of Britain; the third is not so described. All are included among the bishops of the Galliae, that is, of the province of the Roman Empire so called. Three may not sound a large number, but as a question of proportion it is in fact large[28]. Thirty-two or thirty-three bishops, in all, signed the decrees of the Council. Of these, seven were from Italy and the islands, ten from Africa, eleven from what we call France, three from

Britain, and two from elsewhere. The large number of bishops from Africa will surprise no one who knows the prominence of the African Church in the early times, the large number of its bishoprics, the area which it covered. It was the birthplace and home of Latin Christianity, while the Roman Church was still practically a Greek Church. In Africa, not in Italy, the Latin version of the Scriptures was first made.

The principal French bishoprics represented at Arles were Marseilles, Vienne, Lyons, Bordeaux, Trèves, Rheims, and Rouen. In such company it is quite sufficient for us to find York and London, and a see which is understood to be Caerleon; the three bishops thus representing the whole of the island except Caledonia, and occupying what may well have been regarded as the three metropolitical sees, north, south, and west. This coincided fairly well with the re-arrangement of the Roman province of Britain shortly before this time. I venture to suggest that the dates I gave just now, of the foundation of bishoprics in Belgic Gaul, appear to shew some considerable advance in the years about 280, and that from 260 to 280 may have seen the commencement of British episcopacy.

The records of the signatures at the Council of Nicaea in 325 are, as is well known, not in such a state as to enable us to say that British bishops were present. But considering their presence at Arles, the first of the Councils, and the interest of Constantine in Britain and his intimate local knowledge of its circumstances; considering, too, the very wide sweep of his invitations to the Council; it is practically certain that we were represented there. At the Council of Sardica, in 347, only the names of the bishops are given, not their sees. But fortunately the names of the bishops are grouped in provinces. The province of the Gauls—that is, Gaul and Britain—had thirty-three bishops present. I think that any one who has studied the dates of the foundation of the French bishoprics will allow that to make up thirty-three bishops in 347, several British bishops must have been included. At the Council of Rimini, in 359, there were so many British bishops present that three were singled out from the rest of their countrymen as being so poor that they accepted the Emperor's bounty for their daily support, declining a collection made for their expenses among their brother bishops. The others, who could do without the Imperial allowance, refused it as unbecoming.

In the year 358 or 359, in preparation for this Council of Rimini, a treatise of great importance was addressed to the bishops of the British provinces, among others. This was the treatise of Hilary, bishop of Poitiers, on the Synods of the Catholic Faith and against the Arians. He wrote at a very anxious time, when he was himself in exile for the faith, and when he earnestly desired that his orthodox colleagues should take a broad view, so as not to keep out of their communion any who could properly be included. He addressed his treatise to the bishops of Germany, Gaul, and the British provinces. He wrote as to men thoroughly familiar with the very subtle heresy that was dividing the world, men who were thoroughly sound on the point in dispute, but inclined perhaps to be rather unflinching on a point on which he desired to make some concession—concession in terms, not in substance. He specially urged them not to press as vital one single phrase, not to reject as fatal another. For, as he pointed out, each phrase could be used with a sound meaning, either could be used unsoundly. Again, he reminded them of the difficulty inherent in attempts to express exactly in one language a difficult technical phrase from another. Hilary, as the first person in Gaul to write ecclesiastical and religious treatises in Latin, instead of the then more familiar Greek, felt this difficulty keenly; as our own Bede did when he tried to put Caedmon's Creation song into Latin. And he warned them against misconceiving the views of others; pointing out that while they suspected the Oriental bishops of doubting the coequality of the Son of God with the Father, the Oriental bishops suspected them of doubting the distinction between the Father and the Son. Hilary had been, before his conversion to Christianity, a highly-trained and cultured official of his Gallo-Roman city, and he wrote this treatise with force and insight on very difficult subjects. It was a compliment to the bishops of any church that such a document should be addressed to them. We learn in the sequel that Hilary's views of comprehension prevailed; but we have no means of determining what was the share of the British in this result. I need probably not go further in the records of British connection with ecclesiastical events on the continent.

It may have seemed to you rather barren, this talk of Councils. But it is in reality far from being barren talk. It shews us the representatives of the British Church in the full swim of ecclesiastical affairs; summoned as a matter of course to the greatest councils; addressed as a matter of course by the greatest writer of their quarter of the world; taking their share in the settlement of the most subtle and vital points of Christian faith and practice. At Arles, they dealt with the question, so practical after Diocletian's recent persecution, how men were to be re-admitted to the Church, who in time of persecution had fallen away. They decided, further, one of the gravest questions they could have had to decide, whether baptism in the name of the blessed Trinity was valid baptism, even though a schismatic had administered the rite. Their decision was against re-baptism in such cases, a fact of which I may have time to remind you when I speak of some of the practices of the British Church; admission by the laying on of hands was to suffice. They also determined that Easter must be kept everywhere on one and the same day, again a fact which reappears very prominently in their later history. At

Nicaea, they dealt with the greatest question that ever stirred the Church of Christ, the question of the coequal deity, the oneness of nature, of the Son with the Father; and they laid down a rule for observing Easter, from which their descendants 350 years later accused the Roman Church of having departed. At Sardica they asserted the innocence of St. Athanasius; and gave authority to Julius, Bishop of Rome, to receive appeals from a province, if a bishop was dissatisfied with a decision of his synod. Their descendants were too busy with the inroads of barbarians and the subtleties of heretics, to pay much heed to the amusing exposure by the African Church of the Popes Zosimus, Boniface, and Celestine, 417-432, for quoting this Sardican Canon as a Canon of Nicaea, with "Julius" altered to "Sylvester" to make the name fit the forged date. The difference between calling it a Nicene Canon and calling it Sardican may seem little more than a question of a right name and a wrong. But its effect was tremendous. It added the greater part of the known world to the sphere of influence of the Bishop of Rome. For the Sardican Canons were passed by the Western bishops, after the Easterns had left Sardica, and could bind at most only the West. The Canons of Nicaea were binding on the whole of the Christian world. The sarcastic comments of the African Church, in their letter to Celestine, at the close of the controversy, should have had more effect in checking such proceedings than it had. At Rimini the British upheld the coequal deity of the Son; and when the Arian Emperor compelled the signature of a heterodox creed, the bishops of the provinces of Gaul gathered themselves together on their way home, and re-asserted their Catholic belief. Time after time, from Constantine onwards, the unswerving orthodoxy of the British was the subject of special and favourable comment. They were, as I began by saying, in the full swim of ecclesiastical affairs; and they held a position of recognised importance with dignity and effect.

Nor was the journeying of British Christians limited to attending Councils. A historian writing in 420, of the time before 410, says that from East and West people were flocking on pilgrimage to the Holy Land, from Persia and from Britain. And Theodoret, writing of the years about 423, says that many went to the Holy Land from the extreme West, Spaniards, and Britons, and the Galatae who dwelled between them.

We now come to a time when two natives of these islands played a large part —one of them, a very large part, in the origin the principal part—in the great theological controversy of the Western Church, a controversy which touched the East too, but less pointedly. Pelagius and Coelestius enunciated the views on the nature of man, and the operation of the grace of God, which were combated with vehemence by two of the leading men of the West, Augustine and Jerome. From that day to this the controversy has never died out. When the first beginnings of the theory of transubstantiation were heard, this Pelagian controversy divided those who opposed the new idea. Duns Scotus and Thomas Aquinas, in their turn, differed on this point, as Pelagius and Augustine did. The Franciscans and the Dominicans took respectively the views of those two great schoolmen. The Jesuits and the Jansenists of Louis XV's time shewed a like cleavage. Wherever you find Calvinistic views held and combated, there you have in fact the controversy which was started by our countrymen. Calvin declared that every man is predestined to life or to death, from before the foundation of the world. Pelagius maintained the freedom of will and action of every man; his power by nature to turn and come to God; his natural independence, so to speak.

One of the two great opponents of Pelagius, Augustine of Hippo, says that Pelagius was a Briton. The name is Greek, and means "of the sea," "belonging to the sea," and hence his native name has been supposed to be Morgan, sea-born: that, however, is only a guess. The other writers who were his contemporaries call him a Briton. His second principal opponent, Jerome, says that he was by birth one of the Scots, neighbours of the Britons. This meant in those times, and for some centuries after, a native of Ireland, whether living in Ireland or settled in the northern parts of Britain, if any Scots were settled there so early as 370, which was about the date of his birth. It is, however, quite as likely that Jerome is speaking not of Pelagius, but of his companion Coelestius, whom all allow to have been an Irishman. Whichever he means, he is not civil, as he seldom was in controversy. He describes his opponent as "a huge fellow, stuffed to repletion with Scotch porridge," a most disrespectful way of speaking of porridge. Pelagius was a layman, and a monk. About 400 he went to Rome, and he remained there till the shadow of Alaric's siege began to fall upon the city. In those eight years he lived an exemplary life. He urged upon others the necessity of so living, and the uselessness of religious observance combined with laxity of life. It is easy to see how this admirable line of teaching might be diverted, by the pressure of controversion, into a declaration that all men could, if they pleased, so live; that it was a matter of will, not of grace, a man's turning to God and living as a believer should live. This was quite different from the controversy between faith and works, which some have believed to exist between St. Paul and St. James. It was the controversy between the necessity of the grace of God for a man to live as he should, and the comparative subordination of grace to the sufficient power of the will of man. Pelagius held that if the will was not free, man was a mere puppet: if the will was not free, man was not responsible. From this position, which is one side of a great truth, he passed to the denial of the need for God's grace, that is, he denied the other side of the same great truth; or he so defined grace as to make it a mere matter of suitable circumstances.

A great controversy on a great subject can scarcely stop short at its first limits. Other points rise, unexpected results follow. I venture to say that it is impossible to go on pressing one side of this great and lasting controversy on the freedom of the will, to the disregard of the other side, without arriving at results which shock the reverent common sense of the devout Christian.

It is clear, for example, that when Pelagius asserted the freedom of man's will to turn to God, he denied the Catholic doctrine of original sin, and denying that, he denied so far the need for baptism. Indeed he taught directly, it was in fact the key of his position, that when man sinned he sinned after the example which Adam had set, not because he had received the taint of sin by his descent from Adam. When pressed on this question of the need of baptism, he allowed that there was the need, but he put it on a different basis from that which his opponents took. It was not necessary for salvation, he maintained; but for those who desired to reach the full Christian heaven, a state different from that of ordinary salvation, for them it was necessary. Entrance to that higher order of the heavenly life was not to be obtained without baptism. When pressed again, on the question of the need for the operation of the grace of God, he allowed that there was that need. But he explained that when he said God's grace must be given in order that a man might turn to God, he meant that the man must be set in a position and under conditions and with surroundings which rendered it natural and likely that he should so turn. It seems clear, further, that the Pelagian view of the position and nature of man in respect to God is inconsistent with the doctrine of the Redemption wrought by Christ. That great sacrifice is rendered unnecessary, if the views of Pelagius are accepted. Men could, so to speak, turn to God and be saved without the Atonement. It is only fair to say that the extreme view on the opposite side seems to be equally inconsistent with this vital doctrine. If it be true that each man is predestined absolutely to life or to death, whether before the fall of Adam or as the immediate consequence of that fall, it would appear that not all the Atonement of Christ can add one single soul to them that shall be saved.

My object is to speak of Church History, not of doctrine. But this Pelagian question is the most important fact in the history of the British Church; and unless these few words were said to bring out the extreme gravity of the matter in dispute, the episode would not appear to fill the important place it does in fact fill.

With Pelagius himself we have but little to do. He spent his life far from his native shores; he propounded his views in Rome and Carthage and Palestine, not in London and York and Bangor. But the history of what happened to him and his views in those distant parts is so curious—if one may say so, so comical—and the evidence it affords of the importance of the controversy is so great, that I must say a little about it. We shall find in it, I think, an explanation of the course taken by the British Church.

At Rome Pelagius met Coelestius, a Scot—that is, a native of Ireland—and Coelestius became a devoted champion of his views, publishing them in a more definite form than Pelagius himself adopted. These views were condemned at a Council held at Carthage in 412. A Council at Jerusalem in 415 heard the explanations of Pelagius and did not condemn him. A Council at Lydda in the same year fully accepted his explanations, to the great wrath of Jerome. Carthage then took the matter up again, and requested that Pelagius should be summoned to return to Rome, and the whole matter be fully inquired into there, the controversy being one affecting the West and not the East. To enable the Bishop to form an opinion on the views of Pelagius, they sent him a copy of one of his books, with the worst passages marked. Innocent, the Bishop of Rome, gladly received this request, treating it as a request for his authoritative verdict, which it was not. He replied in three letters dated January 27, 417. He began each with a strong assertion of the supreme authority of his see, and many expressions of his satisfaction that the controversy had been referred to him for final decision. The Bishop was clearly not to the manner born. These were not the sayings of unconscious dignity, of unquestionable authority. He did protest too much. The book of Pelagius forwarded to him he pronounced unhesitatingly to be blasphemous and dangerous; and he gave his judgement that Pelagius, Coelestius, and all abettors of their views, ought to be excommunicated.

Nothing could be more clear. But, unfortunately for the consistency of official infallibility, Innocent died six weeks after writing these letters, and Zosimus succeeded him. Coelestius and Pelagius between them were too much for Zosimus. Coelestius came to Rome. He argued with Zosimus that the points in dispute lay outside the limits of necessary articles of faith, and declared his adherence to the Catholic faith in all points. Pelagius did not come, but he wrote to Zosimus. Zosimus declared the letter and creed of Pelagius to be thoroughly Catholic, and free from all ambiguity; and the Pelagians to be men of unimpeachable faith, who had been wrongly defamed. Augustine appears to imply that in his opinion Zosimus had allowed himself to be deceived by the specious and subtle admissions of the heretics.

Zosimus did not rest satisfied with that. He wrote to the African bishops, vehemently upbraiding them with their readiness to condemn, and declaring that Pelagius and his followers had never really been estranged from Catholic truth. Far from accepting his decision or his rebukes, the Africans, who enjoyed a successful tussle with a Pope, sent a subdeacon with a long reply. Zosimus, in acknowledging their letter, wrote in extravagant terms of the dignity of his own position as the supreme judge of religious appeals, and, quaintly enough, hinted at the possibility of reconsidering his decision. The Africans did not wait. They met in synod, 214 bishops or more, and passed nine canons, anathematizing the Pelagian views. The Emperors Honorius and Theodosius banished Pelagius and Coelestius from Rome. What was Pope Zosimus to do, under these singularly trying circumstances? These men, thus banished from Rome, he had declared to be men of unimpeachable faith, wrongly defamed, never estranged from Catholic truth. He dealt with the matter in this way. He wrote a circular letter, declaring that the Popes inherit from St. Peter a divine authority equal to that of St. Peter, derived from the power which our Lord bestowed on him; so that no one can question the Pope's decision. He then proceeded to censure, as contrary to the Catholic faith, the tenets of Pelagius and Coelestius, specially censuring some of Pelagius's comments on St. Paul which had been laid before him since his former decision. He ordered all bishops, in the churches acknowledging his authority, to subscribe to the terms of his letter on pain of deprivation. In Italy itself, Rome's own Italy, eighteen bishops protested against this change of front, and were deprived of their sees under the authority of the civil power.

Of course all men, however exalted their position, are liable to these sudden changes, whether pressed by external circumstances or impelled by inward conviction. And men who have themselves known what it is to be tried in any such way, on however humble a scale, are inclined rather to feel with them than sharply to condemn them; especially when, as in this case, their second thoughts are best. But if they are to be treated thus, with kindly judgement not unmixed with sympathy, they must not herald their change of view with statements that they have a divine authority, equal to that of St. Peter, and that no one can question their contradictory decisions.

To come nearer home after this long digression, which yet is not really a digression from the British point of view. The views of Pelagius had considerable success in Gaul, and gave a good deal of trouble there. In Britain their success was alarmingly great. The bishops and clergy were unable to make head against the wave of heresy. Whether there was anything, in the independence of the position claimed by Pelagius for man, which specially appealed to the nature of the Britons and their Celtic congeners; anything in the claim of each individual to be good enough in himself, if he pleases to be good enough; which harmonised with the opinion those races had—dare I say have?—of themselves; these are questions to which I cannot venture to give an answer. There the fact remains, that Pelagianism did appeal very strongly to the temperament of those who then dwelt in our land. And coupled with this is the fact, that, however orthodox the clergy and bishops might be, and however well versed in the great controversy in which in the previous century they had played their part, the subtleties of this new controversy, initiated as it was by one of their own or kindred race, springing up from their own nature and appealing to the nature of their people, were too much for them—as indeed they had been for Pope Zosimus. Agricola was the name of the man who acted as the apostle of the Pelagians in the home regions, the son, we are told, of a bishop of Pelagian views.

What our predecessors may have lacked in subtlety, they more than made up in practical common sense. If they could not grapple with the heresy themselves, they sent for those who could. They applied to their nearest ecclesiastical neighbour, the Church of Gaul, to which no doubt they looked partly as their mother and partly as their elder sister. The account of their application and the response it met with comes to us from a life of Germanus, Bishop of Auxerre, the person chiefly concerned, written by special request forty years after his death by an eminent person, and published on the request of the then Bishop of Auxerre. When the application reached the heads of the Gallican Church, a numerous synod was called together, and Germanus, Bishop of Auxerre, and Lupus, Bishop of Troyes, were appointed to visit Britain. The manner of treating the heresy had been forced upon the attention of the Gallican prelates by their own experiences. At that very time semi-Pelagianism was rife in the south of Gaul, about Marseilles, and it continued in force there for a long time, another fellow-countryman of ours, Faustus the Briton, imbuing even the famous monastery of Lérins with this modified form of the heresy. To concert measures for dealing with the south of Gaul, Prosper of Aquitaine, a monk and probably a layman, afterwards secretary to Pope Leo the Great, went to Rome about two years after this to consult the Pope, and from Celestine he no doubt heard what he repeated or embellished twenty-five years later. He tells us that the Pope took pains to keep the "Roman island" Catholic, referring of course to the long occupation of Britain by the Roman troops, at this time abandoned. In another passage, whose genuineness has been questioned, Prosper says that Celestine sent Germanus in his own stead to Britain. Prosper was certainly in a position to receive from the best-informed source an account of what was done; but the Gallican Church appears to have known nothing of this sending of Germanus by Celestine. Prosper's inclination to magnify the importance of the Popes has been referred to already[29]; and we may take it as certain that if such an unparalleled step as going himself or sending some one in his stead, a forecast of Gregory's action, had been attempted or taken by the Pope, we should have heard of it in the records of Gaul or in the life of Germanus. The successor of Germanus would have known of it. That Celestine had known at the time what was going on, and that he felt and probably expressed warm approval, we may regard as certain too. I must defer, to an opportunity in my third lecture, remarks which I wish to make on what may seem an ungenerous questioning of these assertions of benefits conferred by Rome.

In 429, then, the Gallican prelates came to Britain. They had a very rough crossing, and a story, rejected with scorn by quite modern writers, is told of a miracle wrought by Germanus. He stilled the storm by pouring oil upon the sea in the name of the Trinity. We now know that if they had oil on board, and knew how to use it, the stilling of the waves was done; without miracle, but with not the less earnest trust in the watchful care of God[30].

It was on this journey to Britain that Germanus and Lupus saw at Nanterre a little girl aged seven, and prophesied great things of her. Her name was Genofeva, and she became the famous Ste. Geneviève. In these days when people coquet with the principles of revolution and shut their eyes to its realities, it may be well to add that her coffin of silver and gold was sold in 1793, and her body burned on the Place de Grève, by public decree.

When they got to work in Britain, they proceeded on a definite plan. Some sixty or seventy years before, Hilary, the Bishop of Poitiers, dealing in Gaul with the great heresy which preceded this, had found it of great service to go about from place to place and collect in different parts small assemblies of the bishops, for free discussion and mutual explanation. He found that misunderstandings were in this way, better than in any other, got rid of, and differences of opinion were reduced to a minimum. Germanus and Lupus dealt with the people of Britain as their predecessor had dealt with the bishops of Gaul. They went all over, discussing the great question with the people whom they found. They preached in the churches, they addressed the people on the highroads, they sought for them in the fields, and followed them up bypaths. It is clear that the visitors from Gaul could speak to the people, both in town and in country, in their own tongue, or in a tongue well understood by them. No doubt the native speech of Gaul and that of Britain were still so closely akin that no serious difficulty was felt in this respect. They met with success so great that the leaders on the other side were forced to take action. They felt, so the biographer tells us, not that his is likely to be convincing evidence as to their feelings, that they must run the risk of defeat rather than seem by silence to give up the cause. They undertook to dispute with the Gallicans in public. The biographer is not an impartial chronicler. The Pelagians came to the disputation with many outward signs of pomp and wealth, richly dressed, and attended by a crowd of supporters. Why should the biographer thus indicate that the Pelagian heresy was specially rife among great and wealthy and popular people? Perhaps it may be the case, that, with imperfectly civilised people, a position of wealth and distinction tends to make men less humble in their view of the need of the grace of God. Besides the principals, we are told that immense numbers of people came to hear the dispute, bringing with them their wives and children; coming, in the important phrase of the biographer, to play the part of spectator and judge. That is the first note we have of the function of the laity in religious disputes in this land of ours. It is a pregnant hint. The disputants were now face to face. On one side divine authority, on the other human presumption; on one side faith, on the other perfidy; on one side Christ, on the other Pelagius. The description is Constantius's, not mine. The bishops set the Pelagians to begin, and a weary business the Pelagians made of it. Then their turn came. They poured forth torrents of eloquence, apostolical and evangelical thunders. They quoted the scriptures. The opponents had nothing to say. The people, to whose arbitration it was put, scarce could keep their hands off them; the decision was given by acclamation, against the Pelagians.

Where did this take place? Certainly not far from Verulam, for Constantius goes on to say that the bishops hastened to the shrine of St. Alban, which at the request of Germanus was opened, that he might deposit there some relics which he had brought with him. He took away, in exchange, some earth from the actual spot of the martyrdom. Presumably the disputation took place somewhere near London, on the road to St. Albans; perhaps at Verulam itself.

The British Church was thus saved from enemies within; but enemies without soon had it by the throat. There were no Roman troops to guard the northern wall, to guard the Saxon shore. The Roman troops had gone, and with them the flower of the British youth[31]. From north and east the barbarians poured in upon the Britons, pell mell. Gildas, crying bitter tears, and using bitter ink, in his Welsh monastery, tells us of the weakness and the follies of the British and their kings, of the cruelties of the barbarous folk. We see in his pages the smoke of burned churches, the blood of murdered Christians. Matthew of Westminster tells us that the churches that were burned had the happier fate. In thirty cases churches were saved and made into heathen temples, the altars polluted with pagan sacrifice. But the Saxons and Angles made way so slowly that it is certain they met with a much sturdier opposition than Gildas credits his countrymen with. Strive as they would, however, and did, the Britons gradually gave way. Thus, and thus only, can we fill the dreary void in British history, which we know as the first hundred and fifty years of the Making of England.

This brings us very near to the end of our period. Not of our subject; for in my concluding lecture I have to deal—with sad scantness—with the Christian Church in other parts of these islands, before and at the coming of Augustine.

In the twenty years immediately preceding the arrival of Augustine, the long line of British Bishops of London came to an end. It has been a subject of remark, and of moralising, that Theonus, the last bishop, lost heart and fled just when the chance was coming for which it is presumed that he had been waiting, the actual beginning of the conversion of the English. But remarks of this character are misplaced; they disregard—or are ignorant of—the political facts of the time. Theonus of London was a British bishop in a British city. London had not fallen. Most difficult of access in the then state of land and water, of marsh and mud, whether from north or south or east or west, it held out to the last. The earliest date that can be assigned to its fall is about the year 568, and a date so early as that is only given to account for Ethelbert's being able to take his army from Kent to Wimbledon without interruption from London. But for that, and there may be other explanations of it, it is quite possible to put the taking of London by the East Saxons a few years later. But it is not necessary for our purpose. The date of the flight of Theonus has been said to be 586. It is probable that this is about the date of Ethelbert's vigorous action northwards, by which he made himself over-lord of his East Saxon neighbours and of London their most recent conquest, which they appear not to have occupied for some years after its fall. The political and administrative changes, due to this expansion of the power of Kent, may well have made ruined London no longer a possible place of residence, and of work, for a Christian Briton so prominent in position and office as the Bishop of London must always have been. It seems probable that Matthew of Westminster was not far wrong when he wrote that in 586 Theonus took with him the relics of the saints, and such of the ordained clergy as had survived the perils, and retired to Wales. Others, he says, fled further, to the continental Britain. Thadioc of York, he adds, went at the same time. In some parts, as for instance about Glastonbury, the British Christians remained undisturbed by the English for sixty or seventy years longer[32].

A year or two ago, when we set up the list of Bishops of London in the south aisle here, there was at first an inclination in some quarters to criticise the decision at which we arrived as to the bishops of the British period. But the explanations kindly given by those who approved our action soon put a stop to that. There is a list of Archbishops of London before Augustine's time, beginning about the year 180 and ending with Theonus, whose date may be put about 580. In those four centuries, sixteen names are given, a number clearly insufficient for 400 years. The names are specially insufficient in the later part of the time, only four being given between 314 and 580. This is rather in favour of the four names being real; for it is evident that if people were inventing names, they might as well have invented twenty, while they were about it, instead of only four, for 260 years[33].

The traditions of York do not supply any long list of bishops, continuous or not. Eborius, at Arles in 314, is the first named. And there are only three others, each of whom has a date with Matthew of Westminster, Sampson 507, Piran 522, Thadioc 586. York probably fell as early as the date assigned to Sampson; who, by the way, was created Archbishop of York by the forgers of the twelfth century, to back up an ecclesiastical claim on the continent.

The decision at which we arrived in respect of the London list was to give one name only, that of Restitutus, putting a row of dots above him and below him, to shew that there were British bishops before him, probably very few, and British bishops after him, certainly many. Restitutus signed the decrees of the Council of Arles, as Bishop of London, in the year 314. That is sure ground; and in a list of bishops, set up officially in the Cathedral Church, nothing less solid than sure ground should be taken.

As to the British Bishops of London being styled archbishops, there is no evidence for it. Our famous Dean Ralph (A. D. 1181), no mean historian, left on record his view that there were three archbishoprics[34] in Britain—London, York, and Caerleon—which last, he said, corresponded to St. David's. Whether Gregory had some information that has since been lost, respecting the ecclesiastical arrangements which had existed here, we cannot say; but it is a curious coincidence, explicable perhaps by the mere importance of the two places, that he directed Augustine to make arrangements for a metropolitan at London, with twelve suffragans, and a metropolitan at York with twelve suffragans. The complete arrangements, as set out by Gregory when he sent an additional supply of missionaries to Augustine, of whom Mellitus was one, were as follows. Augustine was told to ordain in various places twelve bishops, to be subject to his control, so that London should for the future be a metropolitan see; and it appears that Gregory contemplated Augustine's occupying as a matter of course the position of Bishop of London[35]. He was to ordain and send to York a suitable bishop, who should in like manner ordain twelve bishops and become the metropolitan. The northern metropolitan was to be under Augustine's jurisdiction; but after Augustine's death he was to be independent of London, and for the future the metropolitan who was senior in consecration was to have precedence[36]. This takes no account of the bishops existing in what we call Wales and Cornwall. Gregory specially declared that those bishops, then at least seven in number, were subject to Augustine. It is impossible that these seven were to be included among the twelve suffragans of London, for with Rochester and Canterbury that would leave only three bishops for the whole of the rest of the south of England. That the tradition of British times, and a part of the scheme actually laid down by Gregory, should be carried out in our time, would be I think an excellent thing. An Archbishop of London, with some half-dozen suffragans, with dioceses and diocesan rank, in districts of this great wilderness of houses, would be a solution of some very difficult problems.

There were two names in the traditional list which it was thought we might at least have included along with Restitutus. One was that of the last on the list, Theonus. But the evidence for him, though quite sufficient for ordinary purposes, was not of the highest order. The other was that of Fastidius, the last but two on the list. His date—for he was a real and well-known man—was much earlier than that position would indicate, for he was described, among illustrious men, by a writer who lived a full century before Theonus, the last on the list. This writer, Gennadius of Marseilles, informs us that Fastidius was a British bishop. One important manuscript has, in place of this, "Fastidius a Briton," as if his being a bishop was not certain. In any case there is nothing to connect him with the bishopric of London, or with London, beyond the natural assignment to the most important position of a man not specially assigned by the earliest historian. His date is probably about 430 to 450.

This Fastidius is the only writer of the British Church, besides Pelagius if we can properly reckon him as one, whose work has come down to us. I do not know that the early British Christians produced any writers other than Fastidius and Pelagius. Had their records not been destroyed, it might well have been that many a manuscript work of British bishops would have remained till the middle ages and been now in print. Fastidius and Gildas are sufficient evidence of the literary tendencies of the British mind. Indeed, we may credit the Britons of the time of Gildas with having been laborious students, those, at least, who were settled in Wales. Their Celtic cousins had a passion for writing.

We find Gennadius of Marseilles testifying to the soundness of the doctrine of Fastidius, and its worthiness of God. But who shall testify to the soundness of Gennadius? He was a semi-Pelagian; and so it appears was Fastidius, for whose soundness he vouches. Fastidius distinctly quotes from Pelagius, though without mentioning him by name. He uses the phrase which is the keynote of Pelagianism, man sinned "after the example of Adam;" and he describes the manner in which saints should pray, in words which cannot be independent of Pelagius's words on that subject.

Apart from their heretical tendency, the works or work of Fastidius may be taken as containing excellent teaching. He naturally presses most the practical side, the necessity of a good life. "Our Lord said," he shrewdly reminds the reader, "If thou wilt enter into life, keep the commandments; He did not say keep faith only. For if faith is all that is required, it is too much to say that the commandments must be kept. Far be it from me to suppose, that my Lord said too much on any point." One interesting allusion to the state of the country in his time, the Christian settlements here and there in the midst of a heathen population, it may be the Romano-Briton among the unmixed Britons, occurs in a passage full of practical teaching:—"It is the will of God that His people should be holy, and free from all stain of unrighteousness; so righteous, so merciful, so pure, so unspotted from the world, so single-hearted, that the heathen should find in them no fault, but should say in wonder, Blessed is the nation whose God is the Lord, and the people whom He hath chosen for His own inheritance."

LECTURE III.

Early Christianity in other parts of these islands.—Ninian in the south-west of Scotland.—Palladius and Patrick in Ireland.—Columba in Scotland—Kentigern in Cumbria.—Wales.—Cornwall.—The fate of the several Churches.—Special rites &c. of the British Church.—General conclusion.

We are to consider this evening the early existence of Christianity in other parts of these islands, in order that we may have some idea of the actual extent to which Christianity prevailed in England, Wales, Scotland, and Ireland, at the time when Augustine came to Kent.

The Italians appear to have blamed the British Church for its want of missionary zeal. But that only applied to missions to the Angles and Saxons; and I have never quite been able to see how the Britons could be expected to go to their sanguinary and conquering foes with any message, least of all to tell them that their religion was hopelessly false. The expulsion of the Britons from the land of their fathers was too recent for that; the retort of the Saxons too apposite, that at least their gods had shewn themselves stronger than the God of the Britons.

It is a curious fact that we know more of the work of the British Church beyond its borders than at home; and what we know of it is very much to its credit. Somewhere about the year 395, when the inroads of barbarians from the north had become a grave danger, and the territory between the walls had been abandoned by the Romano-Britons, one of the British nation, who had studied at Rome the doctrine and discipline of the Western Church, and had studied among the Gauls at Tours, established himself among the Picts of Galloway and built there a church of stone. The story is that he heard of the death of his friend Martin of Tours when he was building his church, and that he dedicated it to him. This, which after all is a late story in its present form, but is, as I think, to be fully accepted, gives us the date 397; the only sure date in Ninian's history. From this south-west corner of Scotland he spread the faith, we are told, throughout the southern Picts, that is, as far north as the Grampians.

This Christianising of the Picts may not have been very lasting. Patrick more than once speaks of them[37] as the apostate Picts. It did not prevent their ravaging Christian Britain, denuded of the Roman troops. But it had a great influence in another way. The monastery of Whithorn, which Ninian founded, was for some considerable time the training place of Christian priests and bishops and monks, both for Britain, and, especially, for Ireland. The Irish traditions make Ninian retire from Britain and live the later part of his life in

Ireland, where he is certainly commemorated under the name Monenn, —"Mo" being the affectionate prefix "my," and Monenn meaning "my Ninian."

Ninian lived and worked, we are told, for many years, dying in 432, a date for which there is no known authority. That period covers the second, third, and fourth withdrawal of the Roman troops from the northern frontier and from Britain[38]; a time when British Christians might well have said they had more than enough to do at home. Ninian's work has left for us memorials such as no other part of these islands can shew. There are three great upright stones, one at Whithorn itself, and two at Kirkmadrine, that in all human certainty come from his time. They are in complete accordance with what we know of sepulchral monuments in Roman Gaul. Each has a cross in a circle deeply incised, with the member of an R attached to one limb, so as to form the Chi Rho monogram. The Chi Rho is found as early as 312 in Rome and 377 in Gaul, with Alpha and Omega, 355 in Rome and 400 in Gaul. *Hic iacet* is found in 365. The stone at Whithorn itself has *Petri Apustoli* rather rudely carved on it. The two at Kirkmadrine have Latin inscriptions[39] well cut, running apparently from one to the other, as though they had stood at the head and foot of a grave in which the four priests were buried:—"here lie the chief priests"—some say that at that time *sacerdotes* meant bishops—"that is, Viventius and Mavorius" "[Piu]s and Florentius." One of these latter stones has at the top, above the circle, the Alpha and Omega[40]. I ought to say "had," for some years ago a carriage was seen from a distance to drive up to the end of the lane leading to the desolate burying-place, a man got out, went to the stone, knocked off with a hammer the corner which bore the Omega, and made off with it. They are since then scheduled as ancient monuments. There was formerly a third stone, which bore the very unusual Latin equivalent of Alpha and Omega, *initium et finis*, "the beginning and the end." These remains in a solitary place may indicate the wealth of very early monuments we must once have had in this island, long ago broken up by men who saw nothing in them but stones. Time would fail if I were to begin to tell of the recent exploration of the cave known by immemorial tradition as Ninian's cave, and of the sculptured treasures of early Christianity found there. There is in this same territory between the walls, but nearer the northern wall, another memorial of the later British times. It is a huge stone a few miles north-west of Edinburgh, with a rude Latin inscription[41], *In this tumulus lies Vetta, son of Victis*. It takes us to the time when, along with the Picts and Scots who ravaged Britain, we hear for the first time of allies of the ravagers called Saxons. We are accustomed to think of the Saxons as coming first from the south-east and east; but we hear of them first in this region of which we are speaking. As Vetta and Victis correspond to the names of the father and grandfather of Hengist and Horsa, it is difficult to resist the suggestion that in this great Cat Stane, that is, Battle Stone, we have the monument set up by the Romano-Britons, in triumph over the fallen chief of the Saxon marauders. If this is so, the sons of Vetta found the south of the island better quarters than their father found the north, though Horsa, it is true, was killed soon. A great monument bearing his name was to be seen in Bede's time in Kent, and this fact serves to confirm the assignment of the Cat Stane to another generation of his family.

Ninian affords one of the many evidences of a close connection between Britain and Gaul. We should have been surprised if there had not been this close connection; but somehow or other it has been a good deal overlooked. He dedicated his church to his friend St. Martin of Tours. In the Romano-British times a church at the other end of the island, in Canterbury, had a like dedication; and these are the only Romano-British dedications of which we are sure, so far as I know.

In these dedications we may find an interesting illustration of what took place in Gaul, especially in the parts near Britain. There are eighty-six dioceses in modern France, and there are in all no less than 3,668 churches dedicated to St. Martin. There are eight of the eighty-six dioceses which have more than 100 churches thus dedicated, and all of these eight are in the regions opposite to the shores of Britain. Amiens has 148; Arras 157; Bayeux 107; Beauvais 110; Cambray 122; Coutances 103; Rouen 112; Soissons 158. Here again is an instance which shows Soissons prominent in a British connection[42]. No other diocese has more than eighty-four; and only five others have more than seventy. The Christian poet of the sixth century, writing at Poitiers of St. Martin, declares that the Spaniard, the Moor, the Persian, the Briton, loved him. This order of countries is due only to the exigencies of metre. Gaul is not named, because it was the centre of the cult of St. Martin, and there Fortunatus wrote.

Next in order of time, we must turn to the main home of the Celtic or Gaelic Church, the main centre of its many activities, Ireland. As is very well known, Ireland never formed part of the Roman empire; never came under that iron hand, which left such clear-cut traces of its fingers wherever it fastened its grip. Agricola used to talk of taking possession, about the year 80 A. D., but he never went. He had looked into the question, and he thought the enterprise not at all a serious one, from a military point of view; while, as a matter of policy, he was strongly inclined to it. His son-in-law Tacitus tells us this[43], in one of those little bursts of confidential talk which obliterate the eighteen centuries that intervene, and make us hear rather than read what he says. "I have often heard Agricola say that with one legion, and a fair amount of auxiliaries, Ireland could be conquered and held; and that it would be a great help, in governing Britain, if the Roman arms were seen in all parts, and freedom were put out of sight." If this means that Ireland could be seen from the parts of Britain of which he was speaking, we must understand that he spoke of the Britons north of the Solway; and we know that after his operations against Anglesey he passed on to subdue the parts of Wigton and Dumfries, and, two years later, Cantyre and Argyll. Those are the parts of this island from which Ireland is easily visible.

Of course we all know that St. Patrick was the Apostle of Ireland. That puts the introduction of Christianity rather late; the date of Patrick's death, which best suits at once the national traditions and the arguments from contemporary events, being A. D. 493. Those who feel bound to give him a mission from Pope Celestine put his death in 460, rather than face the difficulty of making him live to be 120—or, as some say, 132.

The story of St. Patrick's life is told by many people in many different ways, both in modern times and in ancient. In one of the accounts, known as the Tripartite Life, written in early Irish, we find mention of the existence of Christianity in Ireland before his time. He and his attendants were about to perform divine service in the land of the Ui Oiliolls, when it was found that the sacred vessels were wanting. Patrick, thereupon, divinely instructed, pointed out a cave in which they must dig with great care, lest the glass vessels be broken. They dug up an altar, having at its corners four chalices of glass. Even in the Book of Armagh we find that Patrick shewed to his presbyter a wonderful stone altar on a mountain in this region. This may seem a slight basis on which to found the existence of Christianity before Patrick, but its incidental character gives it importance; and traditions of early times support the conclusion. The whole of an elaborate story of Patrick finding bishops in Munster, and coming to a compromise with them, is a late invention, forged for an ecclesiastical purpose.

There is certainly evidence of an intention to preach Christianity in Ireland before Patrick's time, and this evidence itself affords evidence of a still earlier teaching. In speaking of the visit of Germanus to Britain to put down Pelagianism, the first of two visits as tradition says, I intentionally said nothing about the visit of Germanus's deacon Palladius to Rome. Some writers would not allow the phrases "Germanus's deacon," and "visit to Rome." They say that Palladius was a deacon of Rome; from that he is made archdeacon of the Pope; and from that again a cardinal and Nuncio apostolical. But I shall take him to be the deacon of Germanus, a Gaul by birth and education, though some believe that he must have been himself an Irishman.

The Chronicle of Prosper of Aquitaine, of which we have heard before[44], has in the less corrupt of the two editions the statement that in 431 "Palladius was consecrated by Pope Celestine, and sent to the Scots believing in Christ, as their first bishop." The Scots, of course, then and for some centuries later, were the Irish. It is interesting to us to find Pope Leo XIII, in his Bull restoring the Scottish hierarchy in 1878, gravely taking Prosper to mean that Celestine sent Palladius as the apostle of the Scots in the modern sense of the word, that is, the people of what we call Scotland. Fordun, the chronicler of Scotland, came upon the same rock, and was driven by consequence into wild declarations about the work of Palladius in North Britain. Fordun, however, had the disadvantage of not being infallible.

Prosper of Aquitaine is not a person to be implicitly followed, when the subject is the claims and the great deeds of bishops of Rome. There is a fair suspicion that it was he who credited Eleutherus with the mission to Lucius[45]. His very title, Prosper of Aquitaine, reminds us that Aquitaine includes Gascony. He is suspected of being a romancer. With him, as indeed with many of the evidences of the importance of the action of Rome in early times, great caution is necessary.

Remarks of this kind I do not make from choice; they are forced upon me. It is a pleasure of a very real kind to feel grateful; but when people base upon benefits conferred very large demands and claims, one's feelings of gratitude rapidly and permanently take a very different character. A proverb tells us not to look a gift horse in the mouth. But when there is grave doubt whether the horse ever existed, and when an immense price is afterwards demanded for the gift, proverbs of that kind do not appeal to us very strongly. The claims upon us of mediaeval Rome, mischievous as they were absurd, were based on evidence much of which was so fictitious, that we are more than justified in scanning closely the beginnings of any of the evidence. Time after time one is reminded, in looking into these claims, of the retort of a lay ruler, referring to the forged donation by the first Christian Emperor to the bishops of Rome. Asked by the Pope for his authority for the independent position he maintained, "you will find it," he said, "written on the back of the donation of Constantine."

Nor, again, would it disturb me in the least, if convincing evidence were discovered, in favour of much which I think at best doubtful on the evidence as now known. Benefits conferred lay the foundation of gratitude, not of subservience. The descendants, and representatives, of those who conferred them, have in our eyes all the interest attaching to descendants of benefactors. But when the Popes—say of the Plantagenet times—on the strength of the past or of the supposed past, lorded it over the English people, and carried out of England, every year, to be spent in no very excellent way in Italy, sums of money that would seem fabulous if it were not that no one at the time contested their accuracy, the English people found them, and frankly told them so, an intolerable nuisance. The demands of the Popes were so ludicrous in their shamelessness, that when one of them was read to the assembled peers, the peers roared with laughter. We might perhaps forget such episodes as these. We might forget the abominations which at times have steeped the Papacy and the infallible Popes in earth's vilest vilenesses. We might dream, some of us did dream, as young men, of drawing nearer to communion with the old centre of the Western Church, while maintaining our doctrinal position. It was always the fault of the Roman more than the Englishman that we had to part. And now, late in time, in our own generation, the Roman has cut himself off from us by an impassable barrier, the declaration of the divine infallibility of the man who is the head of his Church. It is to me one of the saddest sights on the face of the earth, a thoroughly estimable and loveable old man, whom one cannot but venerate, made the mouthpiece of ecclesiastics who are pulling the wires of policy, and declared to be the medium of divinely infallible judgement.

It may well have been that Palladius came to Britain with Germanus, and here heard—probably from the Britons of the West—of sparse congregations of Christians scattered about in Ireland; and that he sought authority to visit them, and confirm them in the faith, from some source which the Irish people would not suspect or regard with jealousy. That he had the assent of Germanus we may fairly suppose; that he had the consent and authorisation of Pope Celestine I am quite ready to believe. Pope Celestine, we may remember, was one of the Popes who got into trouble with Africa for persisting in quoting a Sardican Canon as a Canon of Nicaea. He was not likely to hesitate on ecclesiastical grounds when action such as this was proposed to him.

Palladius went, then, about 432, to visit the scattered Irish Christians. There is not a word of his mission being of the same character as that of Germanus to Britain, namely, to attack Pelagianism. He landed in Ireland; and then the several accounts proceed to contradict one another in a very Celtic manner. The two earliest accounts, dating probably not later than 700, agree that the pagan people received him with much hostility. One of the two accounts martyrs him in Ireland; the other says that he did not wish to spend time in a country not his own, and so crossed over to Britain to journey homewards by land, but died in the land of the Britons. Another ancient Irish account says that he founded some churches in Ireland, but was not well received and had to take to the sea; he was driven to North Britain, where he founded the Church of Fordun, "and Pledi is his name there." I found, when visiting Fordun to examine some curious remains there, that its name among the people was "Paldy Parish."

The Scottish accounts make Palladius the founder of Christianity among the Picts in the east of Scotland, Forfarshire and Kincardineshire and thereabouts, Meigle being their capital for a long time. They are silent as to any connection with Ireland. They are without exception late and unauthentic, whatever may be the historical value of the matter which has been imported into them. But all, Scottish and Irish, agree in assigning to the work of Palladius in Ireland either no existence in fact, or at most a short period and a small result. The way was thus left clear for another mission. The man who took up the work made a very different mark upon it.

I shall not discuss the asserted mission from Rome of St. Patrick, for we have his own statements about himself. Palladius was called also Patrick, and to him, not to the greater Patrick, the story of the mission from Rome applies.

Some time after the death of Celestine and the termination of Palladius's work in Ireland, Patrick commenced his missionary labours; and when he died in or about 493, he left Christianity permanently established over a considerable part of the island. That is the great fact for our present purpose, and I shall go into no details. It is a very interesting coincidence that exactly at the period when Christianity was being obliterated in Britain, it was being planted in large areas of Ireland; and that, too, by a Briton. For after all has been said that can be said against the British origin of Patrick, the story remains practically undisturbed.

It is, I think, of great importance to note and bear in mind the fact that Ireland was Christianised just at the time when it was cut off from communication with the civilised world and the Christian Church in Europe. Britain, become a mere arena of internecine strife, the Picts and Scots from the north, and the Jutes and Saxons and Angles from the east and south, obliterating civilisation and Christianity,—Britain, thus barbarously tortured, was a complete barrier between the infant Church in Ireland and the wholesome lessons and developments which intercourse with the Church on the continent would have naturally given. Patrick, if we are to accept his own statements, was not a man of culture; he was probably very provincial in his knowledge of Christian practices and rites; a rude form of Christian worship and order was likely to be the result of his mission. He was indeed the son of a member of the town council, who was also a deacon,—it sounds very Scotch: he was the grandson of a priest; his father had a small farm. But he was a native of a rude part of the island. And his bringing up was rude. He was carried off captive to Ireland at the age of sixteen, and kept sheep there for six years, when he escaped to Britain. After some years he determined to take the lessons of Christianity to the people who had made him their slave. The people whom he

Christianised were themselves rude; not likely to raise their ecclesiastical conceptions higher than the standard their apostle set; more likely to fall short of that standard. In isolation the infant Church passed on towards fuller growth; developing itself on the lines laid down; accentuating the rudeness of its earliest years; with no example but its own.

And not only was the Irish Church isolated as a Church, its several members were isolated one from another. It was a series of camps of Christianity in a pagan land, of centres of Christian morals in a land of the wildest social disorder. The camps were centred each in itself, like a city closely invested. The monastic life, in the extremest rigour of isolation, was the only life possible for the Christian, under the social and religious conditions of the time. And each monastic establishment must be complete in itself, with its one chief ruler, its churches, its priests, and the means of keeping up its supply of priests. There was no diocesan bishop, to whom men could be sent to be ordained, or who could be asked to come and ordain. They kept a bishop on the spot in each considerable establishment; to ordain as their circumstances might require; under the rule of the abbat, as all the members were. Very likely in great establishments they had several bishops. The groups of bishops in sevens, named in the Annals, the groups of churches in sevens, as by the sweeping Shannon at Clonmacnois or in the lovely vale of Glendalough, these, we may surmise, matched one another. We read of hundreds of bishops in existence at one time in Ireland, and people put it down to "Irish exaggeration." But given this principle, that an Irish monastery, in a land not as yet divided into dioceses, not possessing district bishops, must have its own bishop, the not unnatural or unfounded explanation of "Irish exaggeration" is not wanted. In some cases, no doubt, a bishop did settle himself at the headquarters of a district, and had a body of priests under his charge, living the monastic life with him under his rule, and exercising ministrations in the district. But in the large number of cases the bishops were only necessary adjuncts to monasteries over which they did not themselves rule. A presbyter or a layman ruled the ordinary monastery, including the bishop or bishops whom the monastery possessed.

I have dwelt upon this because it is a point often lost sight of, and it explains a good deal. And there is a good deal to explain. When Columbanus and his twelve companions from Ireland burst suddenly upon Gaul in the year 590, they formed a very strange apparition. Dressed in a strange garb, tonsured in a strange manner, speaking a strange tongue, but able to converse fluently enough in Latin with those who knew that language, it was found that some of their ecclesiastical customs were as strange as their appearance and their tongue; so strange that the Franks and Burgundians had to call a council to consider how they should be treated. Columbanus was characteristically sure that he was right on all points. He wrote to Boniface IV, about the time when our first St. Paul's was being built, to claim that he should be let alone, should be treated as if he were still in his own Ireland, and not be required to accept the customs of these Gauls. When Irish missionaries began to pass into this island, on its emergence from the darkness that had settled upon it when the pagan barbarians came, their work was of the most self-denying and laborious character. But contact with the Christianity of the Italian mission, or with that of travelled individual churchmen such as Benedict and Wilfrid, revealed the existence of great differences between the insular and the continental type. We rather gather from the ordinary books that these differences came to a head, so far as these islands were concerned, at the synod of Whitby, and that the Irish church not long after accepted the continental forms and practices, and the differences disappeared. But that is not the effect produced by a more extended enquiry. In times a little later than the synod of Whitby, Irish bishops—I say it with great respect—were a standing nuisance. One council after another had to take active steps to abate the nuisance. The Danish invasions of Ireland drove them out in swarms, without letters commendatory, for there was no one to give due commendation. Ordination by such persons was time after time declared to be no ordination, on the ground that no one knew whether they had been rightly consecrated. There was in this feeling some misapprehension, it may be, arising from the fact of the government of bishops in a monastery by the presbyter abbat, but no doubt the feeling had a good deal of solid substance to go upon. It was reciprocated, warmly, hotly. Indeed, if I may cast my thought into a form that would be recognised by the people of whom I speak, the reciprocators were the first to begin. Adamnan tells us that when Columba had to deal with an unusually abominable fellow-countryman, he sent him off to do penance in tears and lamentations for twelve years among the Britons. There is the curious—almost pathetic—letter of Laurentius and Mellitus, the one Augustine's immediate successor, the other our first bishop of English London, addressed to the bishops and abbats of all Scotia. "They had felt," they said, "great respect for the Britons and the Scots, on account of their sanctity. But," they pointedly remark, evidently smarting under some rather trying recollections, "when they came to know the Britons, they supposed the Scots must be superior. Unfortunately, experience had dissipated that hope. Dagan in Britain, and Columban in Gaul, had shewn them that the Scots did not differ from the Britons in their habits. Dagan, a Scotic bishop, had visited Canterbury, and not only would he not take food with them, he would not even eat in the same house."

It is very interesting to find that we can, in these happy days of the careful examination of ancient manuscripts, put a friendlier face upon the relations between the two churches in times not much later than these, and in connection with the very persons here named. In the earliest missal of the Irish church known to be in existence, the famous Stowe Missal, written probably eleven hundred years ago, and for the last eight hundred years contained in the silver case made for it by order of a son of Brian Boroimhe, there is of course a list—it is a very long list—of those for whom intercessory prayers were offered. In the earliest part of the list there are entered the names of Laurentius, Mellitus, and Justus, the second, third, and fourth archbishops of Canterbury, and then, with only one name between, comes Dagan. The presence of these Italian names in the list does great credit to the kindliness of the Celtic monks, as the marked absence of Augustine's name testifies to their appreciation of his character. Many criticisms on his conduct have appeared; I do not know of any that can compare in first-hand interest, and discriminating severity, with this omission of his name and inclusion of his successors' names in the earliest Irish missal which we possess. It is so early that it contains a prayer that the chieftain who had built them their church might be converted from idolatry. Dagan, who had refused to sit at table with Laurentius and Mellitus, reposed along with them on the Holy Table for many centuries in this forgiving list.

Of a similar feeling on the part of the Britons, when isolated in Wales, Aldhelm of Malmesbury had a piteous tale to tell, soon after 700. "The people on the other side the Severn had such a horror of communication with the West Saxon Christians that they would not pray in the same church with them or sit at the same table. If a Saxon left anything at a meal, the Briton threw it to dogs and swine. Before a Briton would condescend to use a dish or a bottle that had been used by a Saxon, it must be rubbed with sand or purified with fire. The Briton would not give the Saxon the salutation or the kiss of peace. If a Saxon went to live across the Severn, the Britons would hold no communication with him till he had been made to endure a penance of forty days." There is quite a modern air about this pitiful tale of love lost between the Celt and the Saxon[46]. Matthew of Westminster, writing in the fourteenth century, carries the hostility down to his time, in words which leave us in no doubt as to their sincerity. "Those who fled to Wales have never to this day ceased their hatred of the Angles. They sally forth from their mountains like mice from caverns, and will take no ransom from a captive save his head."

Another result of the consideration, which I have suggested, of the date and manner of the Christianising of Ireland, is the probability that the Irish Church and the remains of the British Church had some not inconsiderable differences of practice. This is a point which it would be well worth while to examine closely, but we cannot do it now. Laurentius and Mellitus at first supposed that the Britons and the Scots were the same in their habits; then they supposed that they must be different; then they found they were the same. But this was the habit of hostility to the Italian mission in England, and that can scarcely be classed among religious practices. It is too much assumed that the British Church and the Celtic Church were the same in their differences from the Church of the continent. To take one most important point, while they differed from the Church Catholic in their computation of Easter, they differed from each other in the basis of their computation. The British Church used the cycle of years[47] arranged by Sulpicius Severus, the disciple of Martin of Tours, about 410, no doubt introduced to Britain by Germanus; the Irish Church used the earlier cycle of Anatolius, a Bishop of Laodicea in the third century. The Council of Arles, in 314, had found that the West, Britain included, was unanimous in its computation of Easter, and Nicaea, in 325, settled the question in the same sense. Then came the cycle of 410, of which the British were aware, and not the Irish. Then came another, in this way. Hilary, Archdeacon and afterwards Bishop of Rome, wrote in 457 to Victorius of Aquitaine to consult him about the Paschal cycle. The result was the calculation of a new cycle, which was authorised by the Council of Orleans in 541. It was this newer cycle of which the British Church was found to be ignorant, and their ignorance of it is eloquent proof of the isolation into which the ravages of the invading English had driven them. One of the indications of difference between the Irish and the British Church is rather amusing. When the Irish had conformed to Roman customs, well on in the seventh century, they solemnly rebuked the Britons of Wales for cutting themselves off from the Western Church.

We are not to suppose that the only intercourse with Ireland was through Britain by way of the English Channel. The south of Ireland, at least, was in direct communication with the north-western part of France by sea. When a province of the Third Lyonese was formed, with Tours as its capital, in 394, its area including Britany and the parts south of that, Martin was still Bishop of Tours, and he became the metropolitan. He at once sent into Britany the monasticism which he had founded in Gaul, and it passed thence direct to the south-west corner of Wales. Thence it passed to Ireland. We hear of a ship at Nantes, ready to sail to Ireland. And in Columba's time, when the Saint was telling them of an accident that was at that moment happening in Istria, he assured them that in the course of time Gallican sailors would come and bring the news[48]. This double contact must be kept in mind, when we find the south of Ireland different in Christian tone and temper from the north. It would seem that there were race-differences too, but on that I must not enter.

I am not clear that the Irish Church, as such, had anything to do with missionary enterprise among our pagan English ancestors. Columbanus merely passed through Britain, on his way to do a much more widely-extended missionary work in Gaul than Augustine, his contemporary, did in

England. But it is a very different matter when we come to the great off-shoot from the Irish Church, the vigorous Church whose centre was the island of Hii, its moving spirit St. Columba. Iona—to adopt the familiar blunder which makes a *u* into an *n* in a name all vowels—Iona did indeed pay back with a generous hand all and more than all that Ireland had owed to Britain.

It was in 563 that St. Columba crossed over from Ireland to north Britain, with the wonted twelve companions. He established himself in the island of Hii, the Iouan island, now called Iona. In 565 he went to the mainland, crossed the central ridge of mountains, and made his way to the residence of the king of the northern Picts, near "the long lake of the river Ness," not far from Inverness. Here he found much the same kind of paganism as Patrick had found in Ireland. The king's priests and wise men, here as in Ireland, went by the name of Druids, *Magi* in Latin, and professed to have influence with the powers of nature. Here he worked for some nine or ten years with great success, beginning with the defeat of the Druids in their attempt to prevent his coming, followed soon after by the baptism of the king, who appears to have been a monarch of great power and wide rule. Then Columba devoted himself to his island monastery; and it grew under his hands and those of his immediate successors, till its fame reached all lands. Columba died in 597, the very year in which Ethelbert was converted to Christianity. Thirty-seven years after Columba's death, his successors did that for the Northumbrian Angles which the successors of Augustine had failed to do.

We shall make a very great mistake if we ridicule or under-rate the power of the pagan priests, to whom these stories make reference. Classical mythology treats the gods of Greece and Rome as intensely important beings: and their priests were dominant. We must assign a like position to the gods and the priests of our pagan predecessors. When Apollo was consulted in Diocletian's presence, an answer was given in a hollow voice, not by the priest, but by Apollo himself, that the oracles were restrained from answering truly; and the priests said this pointed to the Christians. And when the entrails of victims were examined in augury on another of Diocletian's expeditions, and found not to present the wonted marks, the chief soothsayer declared that the presence of Christians caused the failure. Just such scenes were enacted, with at least as much of tragic earnestness, when Patrick worsted the Druid Lochra in the hall of Tara, or when Columba baffled the devices of Broichan, the arch-Druid of Brude, the Pictish king.

While Columba was doing his great work, Christianity was re-established by a British king in a part of Britain where it had been obliterated by pagan Britons, that is, in the territory called Cumbria, extending southwards from Dumbarton on the Clyde and including our Cumberland. The king was a

Christian; and the question whether Cumbria should be Christian or pagan was brought to the arbitration of battle. The great fight of Ardderyd, a few miles north of Carlisle, gave it for Christianity in 573, twenty years before the period to which our attention is mainly drawn. Kentigern, a native of the territory between the walls, became the apostle of Cumbria. His mother was Teneu, or Tenoc, and in these railway days she has re-appeared in a strange guise. From St. Tenoc she has become St. Enoch, and has given that name to the great railway station in Glasgow, much to the puzzlement of travellers, who ask when the Old Testament Enoch was sainted by the Scotch[49]. The establishment of Christianity in this kingdom of Cumbria is said by the Welsh records to have had a great result. They claim that the first conversion of the northern section of the Northumbrian Angles, before their relapse, was due to a missionary who was of the royal family of Cumbria; indeed they appear to assert that Edwin of Northumbria himself was baptised by this missionary, Rum, or Run, son of Urbgen or Urien.

It seems probable that the districts of Britain which we call Wales had in Romano-British times only one bishopric, that of Caerleon-on-Usk, near Newport, in Monmouthshire. But as soon as light is seen in the country again, after the darkness which followed the departure of the Romans, we find a number of diocesan sees. The influx of bishops and their flocks from the east of the island no doubt had something to do with this, as had also the territorial re-arrangements under British princes. The secular divisions probably decided the ecclesiastical. Bangor, St. Asaph, St. David's, Llanbadarn, Llandaff, and Llanafanfawr, are the sees of which we have mention, founded by Daniel, Asaph, David, Paternus, Dubricius, and Afan. The deaths of these founders date from 584 to 601, so far as the dates are known. Llanafanfawr was merged in Llanbadarn, and that again in St. David's. These dates correspond well with the traditional dates of the final flight of Christian Britons to Wales, under the pressure of Saxon conquest. We may, I think, fairly regard this as the remodelling of the British Church, which once had covered the greater part of the island, in the narrow corner into which it had now been driven. It is to Bangor, St. Asaph, St. David's, and Llandaff, that we are to look, if we wish to see the ecclesiastical descendants of Restitutus and Eborius and Adelfius, who in 314 ruled the British Church in those parts of the island which we call England and Wales, with their seats or sees at London, York, and Caerleon.

When we come to consider the flight of the Christian Britons before the Saxon invaders, it is worth while to consider how far Christianity really had occupied the land generally, even at the date of its highest development. The Britons were rather sturdy in their paganism. Their Galatian kinsfolk were pagans still in the fourth century, to a large extent. Their kinsfolk in Gaul were pagans to a large extent as late as 350. It seems to me not improbable that a good many of the Britons stayed behind when the Christian Britons fled before the heathen Saxons; and that the flocks whom British bishops led to places of safety, in Britany and the mountains of Britain, may have been not very numerous. If on the whole the fugitives were chiefly from the municipal centres, places so completely destroyed as their ruins prove them to have been, the few Christians left in the country places would easily relapse. But they would retain the Christian tradition; and from them or their children would come such information as that which enabled Wilfrid to identify, and recover for Christ, the sacred places of British Christianity.

We should, I think, make a serious mistake if we supposed that the British Church in Cornwall and Devon was originally formed by fugitives from other parts of the island. The monuments seem to shew that Christianity was established there as well as in other parts of Britain in Romano-British times. Such monuments as we find there and in Wales do not exist in other parts of the island where the British Church existed; and it is an interesting and important question, is that because these parts were unlike the other parts, or is it because in other parts the processes of agriculture and building have broken up the old stones with their rude inscriptions? We now and then come across a warning that the total absence of monumental remains in a place may not mean that there never were any. Many of you would say with confidence that we certainly have not monumental remains from the original cathedral church of St. Paul's, built in the first years of Christianity and burned after the Conquest. But we have. They found some years ago a Danish headstone, with a runic inscription of the date of Canute, twenty feet below the present surface of the churchyard. You can see it in the Guildhall Library, or a cast of it in our library here. I have no doubt there are many such, if we could dig.

But it is of course impossible here to enter upon the evidence of the monumental inscriptions. They deserve courses of lectures to themselves. I may say that the language of the inscriptions connected with the British Church is Latin, while in Ireland the vernacular is used, quite simply at the great monastic centres of Clonmacnois and Monasterboice; markedly Latinised at Lismore, the place of study of the south. In Cornwall the inscriptions are mostly very curt, just "A, son of B," all in the genitive case, meaning "the monument of A, who was son of B." In Wales they are many of them much longer, and some of them in exceedingly bad Latin, certainly not ecclesiastical Latin, almost certainly Latin such as the Romano-Britons may have talked: "Senacus the presbyter lies here, *cum multitudinem fratrum;*" "Carausius lies here, *in hoc congeries lapidum.*" One of the British inscriptions in Wales is charmingly characteristic of the modesty of the race: "Cataman the king lies here, the wisest and most thought-of of all kings."

Cataman, by the way, is identified with Cadfan, and Cadfan in his lifetime told the Abbat of Bangor his mind in very Celtic style as follows (evidently he made a point of living up to his epitaph): "If the Cymry believe all that Rome believes, that is as strong a reason for Rome obeying us, as for us obeying Rome."

The question of the inscriptions is complicated by a very remarkable phenomenon. There are in South Wales, at its western part, a large number of what are called Ogam inscriptions, and in Devon there are one or two[50]. In the south of Ireland there are large numbers. Outside these islands no such thing is known in the whole world. The language is early Gaelic, that is, the monuments belong to the Celtic, not to the British people[51]. The formula is "(the monument) of A, son of B." In Wales the Ogam is frequently accompanied by a boldly cut Latin inscription to the same effect[52], with just such differences as help to shew us how the Ogam cutters pronounced their letters. My own explanation of the Ogam system is that it represents the signs made with the fingers in cryptic speech, used as very simple for cutting on stone when the need for mystery was at an end, that is to say, in all probability, when Druidism was just dying out, and the practice of committing nothing to writing had ceased to be a religious observance. I merely mention these things to add another to the many varied and interesting problems which are forced upon us by a consideration of our fore-elder, the British Church.

It is time to draw towards a conclusion of this hasty scramble over a full field.

If any one asks, where is the old Irish Church now? Dr. Todd, in his Life of St. Patrick (1864), gives in effect the following answer: 'The Danish bishops of Waterford and Dublin in the eleventh century entirely ignored the Irish Church and the successors of St. Patrick; they received consecration from the see of Canterbury; and from that time there were two Churches in Ireland. Then, the Anglo-Norman settlers of the twelfth century ignored the native bishops, on very high authority. Pope Adrian the Fourth, who was himself an Englishman, claimed possession of Ireland under the supposed donation of Constantine, as being an island. He gave it to Henry the Second, charging him to convert to the true Christian faith the ignorant and uncivilised tribes who inhabited it, and to exterminate the nurseries of vices, and—with an eye to business—to pay to St. Peter a penny in every year for every house in the country. It is clear that there was to be no recognition of the old Irish Church. In 1367 the Irish Parliament at Kilkenny enacted the famous Statute of Kilkenny. It was made penal to present any Irishman to an ecclesiastical benefice, and penal for any religious house within the English pale to receive any Irishman to their profession. Three archbishops and five bishops were to excommunicate all who violated the act. These prelates were all appointed by papal provision; some were consecrated at Avignon; their names tell the old story, Galatian biting Galatian, Celt devouring Celt. There were among the excommunicators an O'Carroll, an O'Grada, and an O'Cormacan. And so it came that when the Anglo-Irish Church accepted the Reformation, the old Irish Church was extinct.' My next sentence is quoted exactly from Dr. Todd. "Missionary bishops and priests, therefore, ordained abroad, were sent into Ireland to support the interests of Rome; and from them is derived a third Church, in close communion with the see of Rome, which has now assumed the forms and dimensions of a national established religion."

If any one asks, where is the old Scottish Church now? Dr. Skene in his Celtic Scotland gives in effect the following answer. 'The old Scottish Church was a monastic system. It worked well as long as the ecclesiastical character of the monasteries was preserved. But the assimilation to Rome introduced secular clergy, side by side with the monastic clergy, and this ended in the establishment of a parochial system and a diocesan episcopacy, which still further isolated the old church in its monasteries. Then the monasteries themselves fell into the hands of lay abbats, who held them as hereditary property, and they ceased to be ecclesiastical establishments. These changes occupied the earlier part of the twelfth century. About the middle of that century the Culdees, the sole remaining representatives of the old order of clergy, were absorbed into the cathedral chapters by being made regular canons; and thus the last remains of the old Scottish Church disappeared.' This was chiefly done in David's reign.

The old Cumbrian Church, that is, the Church of the Britons of Strathclyde, of which we have spoken under Ninian and Kentigern, had all but disappeared in the times of confusion and revolution which began with the Danish invasions. The same David who as king brought the old Scottish Church to an end, as earl had reconstituted Kentigern's diocese. The Culdees who had once formed the chapter had quite disappeared, and absorption was unnecessary. Glasgow had given to it in 1147 the decanal constitution of Salisbury, by Bishop Herbert, consecrated by the Pope at Auxerre. About 1133 Whithorn was reconstituted a bishopric, as suffragan to York; and Carlisle was made a bishopric, as suffragan to York. Other parts had gone before. Thus all vestiges of the old British Church of Cumbria had entirely disappeared before 1150.

The old British Church in Cornwall and Devon came to an end in this way. In 884 King Alfred formed in Devonshire a West-Saxon see, and made Asser the Saxon Bishop. Cornwall was made to undergo several changes, and at last, in 1050, was merged in the see of Exeter. It is a matter of very great difficulty to approach to a determination as to where the British see of Cornwall, or of Cornwall and Devon, really was,—or the sees, if there were more than one.

All record has perished.

If any one asks, where is the old British Church of what is now England? the answer is very different. The old Church is living still. The Bishops of the four dioceses of Wales rule it still. There is a curious irony in the historical contrast between 594 and 1894, in calling attention to which I make and mean no political remark. Political remarks in this place, on this occasion, from one who could not if he would, and would not if he could, dissociate himself from membership of a corporate body, with the reticence which that position sometimes enjoins, and who hopes that his audience is very far from being composed of persons of one set of political views only, political remarks would be merely offensive. The contrast is this. In 594, the Christian bishops of Britain had fled before the pagan English and established themselves in Wales, where they gradually gathered endowments for their holy purposes. In 1894, it is a question of the day whether the Christian English will disestablish them and assign their endowments to purposes less holy.

The old British Church of what is now Wales of course exists still in Wales, with a history quite unbroken from the earliest centuries. If we must specially localise it, St. David's probably is its most direct representative. But it is not possible to draw any clear line between the representatives of the Church in Wales before the English occupation of Britain, and the present representatives of those who fled to Wales to escape from the pagan English.

Just one or two remarks on peculiarities of the Church in Britain.

I have spoken of the writings of Fastidius and Gildas, and have accepted as genuine the writings ascribed to St. Patrick. In all of these we find quotations from the Scripture, and they tell us what is very interesting about the version from which they quote. A hundred or a thousand years hence it will be quite easy for those who read—say—the sermon delivered at St. Paul's last Sunday afternoon, to determine whether the preacher used the Authorised or the Revised Version. So we can tell with ease whether a writer about 430, or 470, or 570, used Jerome's Vulgate Version, or the earlier and ruder Latin Version which preceded it. Of that ruder version there were many differing editions—so to call them. Jerome got a number of copies of it, before setting to work, and he found almost as many differing revisions as there were copies.

Now Fastidius, writing about 430, in the time when intercourse with Gaul and Italy was still full, affords clear evidence that he knew, and on occasion used, the Vulgate. But the Vulgate was very new then, and he much more frequently quoted from the older version. Patrick, fifty years later, has indications that he had some slight knowledge of the Vulgate, if indeed these indications be not due to copyists. Instead of advance in knowledge, Patrick's writing shews isolation from the sources of new knowledge. Gildas, on the other hand, 100 years later, but while Britain was all under the heel of the pagan Saxon, and cut off from the Christian world, shews a very clear advance in the use of the newer version, as might be expected from one of the leading men in the great seminary of South Wales. It seems to me that this strengthens the belief that from and after the time of Martin of Tours, South Wales had means of access to continental scholarship by way of Britany, and not through Britain only.

The point of special interest that comes out in all this investigation of the details of differences in quotations, is, that the edition, or recension, of the Old Version, used by British writers, was unlike any now known. It was, so far as we can ascertain, peculiar to themselves.

We learn from Gildas that the British Church had one rite at least peculiar to itself, that of anointing the hands at ordination. The lessons from Holy Scripture, too, used at ordination, were different both from the Gallican and from the Roman use. In the early Anglo-Saxon Church this anointing the hands of deacons, priests, and bishops, was retained; hence it seems probable that other rites at ordination in the early Anglo-Saxon Church, which we cannot trace to any other source, were British. Such were, the prayer at giving the stole to deacons, the delivering the Gospels to deacons, the investing the priests with the stole.

And what of the administration of the Two Sacraments? To their manner of administering the Holy Communion, Augustine did not raise objection. To their Baptism, he did. What, in detail, the objection was, we do not know. It is a very curious fact that the actual words to be used in baptising are omitted in the Stowe Missal, where full directions as to various rites connected with Baptism are given. If we may judge from some correspondence of Gregory at this date with Spain, it was probably a question between single immersion and immersion three times. Gregory, with a freedom of concession in which he more than any one in like position allowed himself, advised the retention of single immersion in Spain, because of the peculiar position of Spain with respect to Arianism. There was, curiously enough, a British bishopric in Spain at that very time.

To speak of the Holy Eucharist, a course of lectures, instead of a sentence in one lecture, might afford space not wholly inadequate. Augustine wrote to Gregory to ask what he was to do, as he found the custom of Masses[53] in the Church of the Gauls (Galliarum) different from the Roman. Gregory replied that whatever seemed to Augustine the most suitable, whether in the Roman use or in that of the Gauls, or in the use of any other Church, that he should adopt; and having thus made a collection of all that seemed best, he should form it into one whole, and establish that among the English. Gregory actually himself added words to the Roman Canon of the Mass, so free did he feel himself to deal with such points. Augustine went so far in this direction of recognising other liturgies, that he told the Britons if they would agree with him about Easter and Baptism, and help him to convert the English, he on his part would tolerate all their other customs, though contrary to his own. Gildas, thirty years before, stated directly that the Britons were contrary to the whole world, and hostile to the Roman custom, both in the Mass and in the tonsure. A very early Irish statement, usually accepted as historical, shews that the British custom of the Mass was different from that which the Irish had from St. Patrick: that this British custom was introduced into Ireland by Bishop David, Gildas, and Docus, the Britons, say about 560; and that from that time till 666 there were different Masses used in Ireland.

The South of Ireland accepted the Roman Easter in 634, and the North in 692; so this date 666 is not unlikely. But it was centuries before the old national rites really died out in Ireland. Malachy, the great Romaniser, Bishop of Armagh 1134-1148, was the first Irish bishop to wear the Roman pallium. He established in all his churches the customs of the Roman Church.

It may be as well to state approximately the dates at which differences of practice disappeared in the several parts of our own island.

The English of Northumbria abandoned the insular Easter in 664.

The Britons of Strathclyde conformed to the English usages in 688; the first British bishop to conform in that district was present at a Council at Rome in 721, where he signs himself "Sedulius, a bishop of Britain, by race a Scot."

Pictish Scotland, and also Iona, adopted the Catholic rites between 710 and 717.

The Britons of North Wales did not conform to the usages adopted by the Anglo-Saxon Church till 768; those of South Wales till 777.

My object in these last cursory remarks has not been, I really need not say, to convey information in detail on the difficult and intricate points to which I have referred[54]. It has been simply this, to shew how very real, and substantial, and fully equipped, and independent, was the Church existing in all parts of these islands, save only the parts of Britain occupied by the pagan Jutes and Saxons and Angles, at the time when Augustine came; came with his monks from Rome, his interpreters from Gaul. I do not say that there were no pagans left then in parts of Scotland and of Ireland and perhaps of Wales, but the knowledge of the Lord covered the earth, save where the English were.

The impression left on my mind by a study of the face of our islands in the year 594, thirteen hundred years ago, is that of the pause, the hush, which precedes the launch of a great ship. The ship is the Church of England. In the providence of God, all was prepared; Christian forces all around were ready to play their part; unconsciously ready, but ready; passively ready, needing to be called into play. There were obstacles enough, but obstacles removable; obstacles that would be removed. The English had been the first to act. They desired to move. They had called across the narrow sea to the Gauls to come over and help them. But there was no voice, nor any that answered. Once in motion, its own momentum would soon carry the ship beyond the need of the aids that helped it move. Who should touch the spring, and give the initiation of motion?

Far away, in Rome, there was a man with eagle eye, who saw that the moment had come. In wretched health, tried continually by severe physical pain, his own surroundings enough to break down the spirit of any but the strongest of men; with all his sore trials, he was never weary of well doing. He was called upon to rule the Church of Rome at one of the very darkest of its many times of trial. Pestilence was rife; it had carried off his predecessor. Italy was overrun by enemies. The celibate life had for long found so many adherents, that defenders of the country were few; children were not born to fill the gaps of pestilence and war. Husbandry was abandoned. The distress was so great, so universal, that the conviction was held in the highest quarters that those were the fearful sights and great signs heralding the end of the world.

And even more than by these secular troubles was he that then ruled the Roman Church tried by ecclesiastical difficulties. Arianism, so far from being at an end, dominant or threatening wherever the Goths and the Lombards were; and where were they not? Donatism once again raising its head in Africa, and lifting its hands of violence; controversies a hundred and fifty years old, about Nestorianism, breaking into fresh life, threatening fresh divisions of the seamless robe of Christ. He thus described the church he ruled:—"an old and shattered ship; leaking on all sides; its timbers rotten; shaken by daily storms; sounding of wreck."

He it was that in the midst of trials much as these, his own ship on the point of foundering, touched the spring that launched the English Church. Moving very slowly at first; seriously checked now and again; brought up shivering once and more than once; the forces round it not playing their part with a will; some of them even opposing; it still went on and gathered way. As time went on, it took on board one source of strength that most had stood aloof; for many centuries the British Church has formed part of the ship's company. And still the ship goes gallantly on, gathering way; the Grace of God, we hopefully and humbly believe, sustaining and guiding it; guiding it, through unquiet seas, to the destined haven of eternal peace and rest.

The man who in the providence of God touched the spring, was Gregory, the Bishop of Rome. Let God be thanked for him.